'A pumpkin. . .' Lloyd said blankly.

'Sally told me Gina's just yelling because babies feel like pumpkins,' Lisa said.

The moan from the labour ward died to nothing. There was absolute silence. Lloyd stared from the child to Sally and back to the child. His lips twitched. Unsuspected laughter lines creased around Lloyd's eyes and his face transformed. The laughter lines deepened, until Sally was almost smiling back. She watched in disbelief as his deep, rich laughter echoed down the corridor.

'That's not what we tell the mothers in natural childbirth classes, Dr Atchinson. . .'

Marion Lennox has had a variety of careers—medical receptionist, computer programmer and teacher. Married, with two young children, she now lives in rural Victoria, Australia. Her wish for an occupation which would allow her to remain at home with her children and her dog led her to begin writing, and she has now published a number of medical romances.

Recent titles by the same author:

DANGEROUS PHYSICIAN
DOCTOR'S HONOUR
PRACTICE MAKES MARRIAGE
STORM HAVEN

ENCHANTING SURGEON

BY
MARION LENNOX

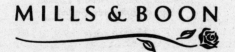

MILLS & BOON

MILLS & BOON, the Rose Device and
LOVE ON CALL are trademarks of the publisher.
Harlequin Mills & Boon Limited,
Eton House, 18-24 Paradise Road, Richmond, Surrey TW9 1SR
This edition published by arrangement with Harlequin Enterprises B.V.

© Marion Lennox 1995

ISBN 0 263 79360 5

*Set in Times 10 on 10½ pt. by
Rowland Phototypesetting Limited
Bury St Edmunds, Suffolk*

03-9510-48885

Made and printed in Great Britain

CHAPTER ONE

'WITH my luck I'll be late for my own funeral.'

Sally Atchinson, surgeon, seized her briefcase with
one hand and a pile of folders with the other, slammed
down the luggage compartment of her car with her
elbow and ran.

Never run in hospital precincts. How many times
had that rule been drummed into her, for heaven's
sake? It couldn't be helped. She had no choice. Sally
was ten minutes late to an interview for the job she
wanted more than anything else in the world.

'Darn cows,' she gasped as she ran. The dairy herd
had blocked half a mile of road, and it had taken her
thirty minutes to get through.

Did she look respectable? The sort of surgeon
Gundowring Hospital just had to have? No way, Sally
thought desperately, but there was no time to comb
her unruly copper curls or powder away despised
freckles. She knew she looked about half her
twenty-nine years.

If Sally Atchinson really worked at her appearance
she could turn herself into the picture of a mature,
poised surgeon, but today she'd been in the car since
dawn and for the last hour had been unable to resist
letting down the hood to feel the salt-laden wind.

Freedom. . . The wind from the sea smelt of freedom, and Gundowring had the most beautiful hospital
in Southern Australia, perched high on a headland
with the sea all around. Oh, she did want this job! A
new start, with heartache and unhappiness solidly
behind her. And she was so late. . .

Sally clutched her belongings close and forced her

5

racing feet to move even faster, then swung round a
corner of the hospital veranda—only to find someone
blocking her path.

She couldn't stop. Sally veered frantically sideways,
her foot caught on the tip of a walking-stick, and she
landed in a tumbled knot of arms, legs and wildly flying
papers.

For a moment the breath was knocked out of her.
Sally sat down hard on her neat bottom and fought
for composure. It didn't come. Composure hardly ever
did when one's skirt was flying up near one's waist
and one appeared to be perched on someone else's
lap. Then, as breath returned, Sally realised what had
happened and she whisked herself sideways with a gasp
of horror.

She'd crashed into a patient. A man with a
walking-stick. . .

Dear heaven. . .

She looked down at the walking-stick lying at her
side and then, fearfully, up at the man sitting beside
her. Sally's bright hazel eyes creased in consternation.

The man looked to be in his early thirties. His
tousled fair hair showed traces of premature grey, and
his face was etched with lines of pain. He'd suffered
a lot, she thought instinctively, knowing the way the
eyes of those often in pain showed subtle changes, and
she cringed inwardly at the knowledge that she'd hurt
him more.

'Oh, my. . . Oh, I'm so sorry. . .' She had done the
unforgivable. Sally reached out a hand to touch his
arm—a gesture to alleviate somehow that look of
suffering—but he shook it off in fury. The look of
pain behind his eyes was fast being replaced with
absolute anger.

'Hand me my stick,' he snapped, and Sally's eyes
widened at the tone of arrogant command. This wasn't
the usual tone of a chronic invalid. Still, she deserved

his anger. Now was hardly the time to ask him to say please, and part of her rejoiced at his arrogance. She couldn't have hurt him too badly if he was talking like this.

She groped behind her for the stick, and placed it in his hands. The man seized it from her without a word, shook off her hands, which sought to assist him to his feet, and struggled to rise.

Sally gazed up at him in dismay as he rose. The man was lean, his strong bone-structure accentuated by his long frame. His wide, strong jaw was clean-shaven and grey-black eyes flashed fury.

'What the blazes. . .?' He managed to find his balance and then stood, leaning heavily on his stick. Anger was emanating in waves, straight at Sally.

He was so darned tall. Sally was slight, and hardly came to more than this man's shoulder when she too struggled to her feet. She looked up at his angry face and tried hard to muster an apologetic smile.

'I'm so sorry,' she repeated. 'I was in a hurry. . .'

'That's no excuse.'

'I know.' She spread her hands helplessly. 'Have I. . .? Have I hurt you? Can I. . .? Can I help you back to your ward?'

Of course she'd hurt him. She could see it in his face—in the way his tanned hand gripped the handle of the stick until his knuckles whitened. It was a stupid question and his face acknowledged her stupidity.

'You haven't done any lasting damage.' His voice was savage with fury. 'But you could have.' He brushed dust from his immaculate linen trousers and white open-necked shirt, and then fixed her with glittering malevolence. 'If you're going to visit someone in this hospital then you obey hospital rules. The rule forbidding running is not emblazoned over the hospital gates because it's assumed people have at least the rudiments of common sense. In your case it seems a foolish assumption.'

Sally took a deep breath, aware that her colour was mounting. She took another, while the man's eyes kept right on boring through the back of her head. Goodness, it was just as well this man seemed on the road to recovery. She wouldn't want him as a patient!

'Look, I really am sorry,' she managed, 'but. . . But I'm running awfully late. If you really are OK I have to meet. . .'

'The boyfriend? He has my sympathy.'

Sally's colour deepened and her temper rose. 'No, not the boyfriend,' she managed, sympathy for the man in front of her fading. It seemed he was well able to care for himself. He might be injured but his tongue was lethal. She stooped to retrieve her papers and stuffed them back into folders, hopelessly out of order. 'If there's nothing I can do for you then I must go. If you could stand aside. . .' The man was blocking the entire veranda.

'You mean you want to run again?'

Sally bit her lip. 'I'm not going to run.' She looked up into his eyes and found her breath coming faster. This man made her feel like a schoolgirl.

Get a hold on yourself, Sally! She was the surgeon, for heaven's sake, and this man was a patient. She needed some authority here.

She needed another six inches. Sally had never regretted her lack of height more. She was dressed as professionally as she ever was without her white coat or surgeon's garb, in a smart summer suit of floral blouse and matching skirt, but this man was looking at her as though she was something that had just crawled from a piece of cheese. A very mouldy piece of cheese!

He stared grimly at her for a long, long moment. His eyes didn't shift from hers and Sally felt something stir, deep within. The beginnings of trouble. . .

'Your name?' he snapped.

It was none of his business. Still, he looked as though he was a long-term convalescent patient, and, if so, then she'd see him again.

'I'm Sally.' She gave a tight little smile that it almost hurt to deliver. Her stomach was doing funny things. 'Sally Atchinson.'

He nodded grimly and then, finally, moved to one side of the path.

'Very well, Miss Atchinson,' he said drily. 'Go and do your visiting. I'm late as well—even later now, thanks to you. Oh, and Miss Atchinson. . .'

Sally had started moving away. Now she stopped and looked back.

'Yes?'

'If I catch you so much as walking fast in this place I'll throw you out—stick or no stick. It would give me considerable pleasure to do just that.'

Of all the arrogant. . .

Sally made herself count to ten as she made her way through the hospital corridors to the boardroom at the rear. The receptionist had directed her and somehow Sally had heard the instructions, but her mind was only partly on her impending interview. The rest was still churning with anger.

Anger? It was she who'd knocked the man down, she reminded herself. So why was she angry?

Maybe not angry. Maybe unsettled. . .

The man's furious eyes floated in front of her and it was all she could do to concentrate on what she was doing and why she was here. The image of the man she'd knocked over blotted out all other thoughts. It was to be hoped that the man was due to be released soon—or maybe he was an outpatient. He'd said he was running late. . .

She cheered up a little at that thought. If he wasn't

an inpatient then she'd never have to see him again—with luck.

So why was her stomach still churning?

The polished wooden doors of the boardroom were straight ahead. Concentrate on the interview, she told herself harshly. Put the man out of your mind and concentrate on getting this job. Concentrate, Sally Atchinson!

It was a panel interview.

Panels were the pits, Sally decided as she sat in the chair and tried to concentrate on her interviewers.

Three doctors sat before her—and another chair sat empty, as if they were expecting someone else to arrive with yet more questions.

Sally was introduced to Dr Struan Maitland, physician, and his wife Gina. Gina was Gundowring's paediatrician, and obviously about to add to Gundowring's population at any minute, but her pregnancy didn't stop her questions being incisive and thorough. The third interviewer, Dr Lesley Maine—a grey-haired obstetrician—sat beside Gina. She had a kind face and a twinkle behind weary eyes which Sally found comforting. Lesley's questions were gentler than Gina's and Struan's, but just as searching.

Sally fielded the questions as best she could, and gradually, gradually relaxed. Slowly the feeling permeated through the interview that she was what these people wanted. They wanted a competent general surgeon, and Sally knew that she was one.

Sally had been one of the youngest ever qualifying surgeons in the state. She loved her work, but she was weary of city practice—especially since her father's death. She wanted a gentler pace, and she wanted to get to know her patients. The endless queues of surgical cases in her huge teaching hospital had become more and more depressing.

So. . . So it seemed she was right for the job. Her freckles and windblown curls were put aside as not important. The three doctors on the panel relaxed, and rose from their seats to make coffee. The grilling was at an end.

'Tell me about the other doctors in the town,' Sally asked as Lesley handed her coffee and a chocolate biscuit. Sally bit into it appreciatively. What had happened to breakfast?

'Well, there are several, of course.' It was Gina Maitland, who was standing awkwardly with her hand to the small of her back, who answered. Her pregnancy was obviously making her uncomfortable. She shook her head as Lesley offered coffee, and Sally saw a trace of what looked like nausea wash over her face. 'For instance, we have another physician, Lloyd Neale, who should be here now.'

'Lloyd said he'd be late,' Lesley volunteered. 'He was running an X-ray of Dave Rowan's foot—but I would have thought he'd be here by now.'

Dave Rowan. . . That might be the man she had run into, Sally thought, and grimaced inwardly. If she'd done more damage, maybe that was why Lloyd Neale was late.

Gina was shrugging. 'We also have several general practitioners and an anaesthetist. We all tend to overlap in duties—we must in such a small community. Our anaesthetist's on long-service leave at the moment—he took the opportunity while we were without a surgeon—so Lloyd's doing anaesthetics. Lloyd did his first part before he decided he preferred his patients awake, so is qualified for general surgery. As well as that——' she grimaced down at her bulge and winced '—we might be without a paediatrician at any tick of the clock.'

'When are you due?' Sally asked.

'S-soon.' The woman before Sally faltered, and her

hand felt the small of her back again. 'I'm starting to think really, really soon. Sally, I'm so sorry. Struan. . .'

Gina's husband was beside her in a moment, the biscuit in his hand falling forgotten to the floor as he reached for his wife. 'Gina. . .'

'I think. . .' Gina's face was set with pain. 'Sally, we're so pleased you're here, and this should be the time to make a fuss of you. But if you don't mind. . .I think I have something really important to do.'

Sally's eyes widened and she started to smile. 'Like having a baby?'

'Like having a baby,' Gina agreed faintly. She bit her lip as a contraction hit, her knees sagging and her husband's hold becoming increasingly necessary. 'Lesley. . .'

Like Sally, the middle-aged obstetrician was smiling with delight. 'About time too,' she said with satisfaction. 'Two weeks overdue! If this little one hadn't made his move today I was going to induce you.'

The contraction deepened in intensity and Gina gave a low moan. Her husband's face tightened as he lifted his wife into his arms.

'Don't worry, Gina, love. Labour ward, Lesley?'

'By the look of that contraction, yes,' Lesley told him. 'Is this your first contraction, Gina?'

Gina shook her head. 'I've been feeling them for a couple of hours,' she confessed. 'This is the first one I haven't been able to disguise. We had Sally's interview, and I didn't want to make a fuss.'

'Oh, of course.' Sally smiled. 'Concentrating on important stuff like asking me about my hobbies when you could be bringing a new person into the world. Get away with you all and deliver this baby.' She opened the door for Struan to carry his wife through.

'Struan. . .' Gina stopped her husband with a whisper.

'Yes, love?'

'Can we offer Sally the job? Before I. . . I mean, I'd sort of like to know. . .'

'We can think of job offers later,' Struan told her, but the girl in his arms shook her head.

'No. I like Sally,' she said stubbornly. 'And I want her on staff.' She pursed her lips. 'Struan Maitland, if Sally isn't offered this job then I'll cross my legs and refuse to have this baby. What do you think, Lesley?'

'You might find the baby has other ideas,' Lesley said drily, but she looked across at Sally and smiled. 'Though I'm with Gina. I think Sally is just the woman for the job. Agreed, Struan?'

'But we haven't consulted Lloyd. Damn, where is the man?' Struan shook his head. 'I suppose you're right though, love,' he told his wife, his eyes smiling fondly down at her. 'The only other competent applicant for the job was a pompous bore. So, consider the job yours, Dr Atchinson.'

'But. . .' Sally shook her head. 'You should consult your other partners.'

'We agreed to a panel of four,' Struan said firmly. 'Even if Lloyd decides against, it's still three against one. So, welcome to the staff, Sally Atchinson. Now, if you'll excuse us. . .'

He turned and strode down the corridor, his precious bundle in his arms.

'Good grief,' Sally said faintly, and behind her Lesley Maine gave a faint chuckle.

'Not your regular interview panel,' the obstetrician agreed. 'It's fine, for all that. We really do need you, Sally, and you seem well-qualified for the job.'

'But Lloyd——'

'Will love you.' Leslie's hand came out to grip Sally's in a gesture of reassurance. 'I know he will. Now, I must go too. I have a feeling I might be required.'

And then she looked over Sally's shoulder down the corridor as the sound of halting footsteps came towards them. 'And here's Lloyd now. I'll have to let you introduce yourself. Gina needs me.'

Her reassuring clasp tightened momentarily, then the middle-aged obstetrician dug her hands deep into the pockets of her white coat and she set off after Struan and Gina. A woman with a job to do—off to deliver Gundowring's newest inhabitant. . .

Sally smiled after her. Then she turned her face towards the approaching footsteps and froze.

'Here's Lloyd', Lesley had said. Lloyd. . . Was this Lloyd Neale, then? Surely not. Not this man limping down the passage towards her, holding a heavy wooden stick for support. He was a patient. He had to be a patient. . .

He wasn't.

'L-Lloyd? Lloyd Neale?' Sally's vision of a lovely future in Gundowring fluttered out of the window as she recognised the man she'd tripped. He was dressed as before, but now had a white coat over his clothes and a stethoscope hanging from his pocket, marking him clearly as a doctor.

The man came to a halt six feet from her. His dark, pain-lined face stilled, frozen of all expression.

'Yes, I'm Lloyd Neale,' he agreed, his voice dripping icicles. 'What on earth do you want now?'

It was all she needed to know. Sally felt the beginnings of tears pricking behind her eyes and held them back with a huge effort. It had seemed so good.

'I'm. . . You know I'm Sally Atchinson,' she whispered. 'I'm here for. . .for the interview.'

'Not for the surgical job?' His brows snapped together in disbelief. 'You're not a surgeon?' His eyes were incredulous.

Anger came to Sally's aid and the threatened tears

receded. 'Because I'm not male and over forty?'

'I knew the job applicant was female.' Lloyd's voice was clipped and cold. 'I didn't expect a child, though.'

A child. . . Sally's eyes flashed. 'I'm twenty-nine,' she flung at him.

'In years,' he scoffed. 'Running about the hospital like an adolescent.'

Sally took a deep breath. 'Dr Neale, I'm sorry I knocked you over,' she said through gritted teeth. 'Very sorry. I shouldn't have run in hospital grounds. I can't do more than apologise, though, and if that's not good enough for you then I'm just going to have to get in my car and go back to Melbourne.'

'I think that might be the best solution all round.'

So that was that. Sally stared up at the man's implacable face and knew that to work with a man like this was impossible. And, in such a small town as Gundowring, to avoid him was not an option. 'Lloyd's doing anaesthetics', Gina had told her. Sally would be surgeon with Lloyd Neale as anaesthetist—a working partnership where trust had to be absolute. Hopeless! To have her closest working partner so antagonistic was out of the question.

So? So Sally had fouled things up. She had hurt this man and wounded his pride, and she had done so by disobeying medical rules. There was no forgiveness in his face. Implacable anger. . .

'Fine,' she said tightly, and turned away. The tears threatened to return but she thrust them back fiercely. She wouldn't let this man see her cry.

'So you two have met!'

Sally didn't look up. She couldn't until she had her face under control, but she recognised Struan's voice as his footsteps sounded down the corridor. He approached them fast. 'Hey, Lloyd, did Sally tell you Gina's in labour?'

'No.' Lloyd's harsh voice still sounded tight with

anger, but he looked up and away from the girl before him. 'That's great, Struan.'

'I'm off home to collect her suitcase.' Struan grinned, excitement sounding in his words. 'The last contractions were two minutes apart. She's been in labour all morning and hasn't told anyone.'

'Dr Maitland. . .' Sally forced herself to look up and made herself speak. Her voice didn't sound her own.

He heard the strain. Struan stopped dead and looked from Lloyd to Sally and back again. 'What's wrong, Sally?'

'Dr Maitland, I want to thank you for offering me the job,' Sally managed. 'But I don't think. . .I'm going back to Melbourne this afternoon. Thank Gina and Lesley for me, will you? And. . .and the best of luck with your baby.'

'What in blazes. . .?' Struan stared down at her and then turned to Lloyd. 'Did you do this? Ten minutes ago we had ourselves a surgeon. And now. . .'

'She's not suitable,' Lloyd said heavily.

'The heck she's not.' Struan was older than Lloyd and it showed. The two men stood facing each other— two opposing forces of implacable will, and Struan was the senior. 'You tell me one reason why she's not suitable.'

'I was late for my interview,' Sally said miserably. 'So I ran. I bumped into Dr Neale and knocked him over.'

'You knocked him over.' Struan turned to look at Sally's face, her eyes bright with unshed tears. She looked about ten, she knew, and she wished the ground would swallow her up. Right now. 'Oh, unforgivable transgression,' Struan continued slowly. 'To knock the great Lloyd Neale over. . .'

'Struan, for heaven's sake,' Lloyd intercepted. 'The woman was running in hospital grounds. I could have been old Mrs Cartwright on her walking-frame.'

'But you weren't,' Struan snapped. He turned back to Sally. 'Have you apologised?'

'Y-yes. Of course.'

'And you swear you won't run in hospital grounds again?' There was a glimmer of a smile in his voice.

Sally swallowed uncertainly. 'I swear.'

'And you promise you won't deliberately knock down our Dr Neale again, unless he deserves it?'

Sally's usually irrepressible smile peeped out. She glanced up at Lloyd and the smile was firmly repressed. Maybe he really did deserve it, she thought. The anger on his face almost warranted another shove.

She choked on a bubble of unexpected laughter and fought to get her face in order. 'I promise.'

'Then there's no problem. Lloyd, is there any other objection to Sally, apart from her tendency to knock people over?'

'I wouldn't know,' Lloyd said tightly. 'I wasn't at the interview. I had to X-ray Dave Rowan's foot.'

'Dave's foot could have waited,' Struan told him. 'Sally was interviewed by myself, Gina and Lesley. We've offered her the job, and unless there's some other objection the appointment sticks.'

'But——'

'No,' Sally interjected. Her laughter had faded as she watched Lloyd's face. 'Dr Maitland. . .'

'Struan.'

'Struan, then. Struan, I can't work with Dr Neale if he feels like this. It won't be possible. I'm sorry, but I think. . .' She spread her hands helplessly. 'I think it might be better if I left.'

'Better for who?' Once again Struan was glaring at Lloyd. 'Better for you, Sally? You want this job, and you want it badly. Better for Gundowring? Your references are impeccable and we need you. Better for Lloyd? Maybe. But Lloyd needs to lighten up.

The other choice is that boring fool we interviewed yesterday, Lloyd. He wouldn't knock you down. He wouldn't run in hospital grounds—I'd be amazed if he could get past a waddle.'

'Look, the woman showed no consideration for hospital patients at all.'

'So, you've never run in hospital precincts?' Struan demanded. 'I know I have—rules or no rules.'

Lloyd's face tightened. 'You know damned well that I can't——'

'Yeah, but you did before your accident,' Struan snapped. 'You were just as impulsive as the rest of us. And now, because you can't, you'll punish anyone who can.' He turned to Sally. 'Our Dr Neale once rode a Harley Davidson—and he was the best dancer in the place. I remember him arranging jazz to be piped through to the nursing home, and vividly recall our Lloyd rocking and rolling with our delighted old ladies. Once——'

'That was when I was young,' Lloyd said stiffly. 'Before. . .'

'Before you lost some movement in your leg,' Struan agreed. 'But it wasn't just movement in your leg you lost, Lloyd. It was your sense of humour. And why you must get yourself engaged to that sour-faced, humourless woman. . .'

'We'll leave Margaret out of this.'

'I'm quite happy to ignore Margaret,' Struan agreed. 'I just wish you would too.' He ran his hand through his hair. 'Look, I have to go. Gina needs me. Sally, you'll stay. Despite Lloyd. Please.'

'I don't. . .' Sally cast a nervous glance up at Lloyd. 'I don't really know.'

'Look, I can't tell Gina you've quit before starting.' Struan cast a harried glance at his watch. 'Tell you what. You're not working at the moment so you could start straight away. Why not give us a month's trial?

If you and Lloyd can't come to some workable relationship by then we'll have lost nothing. You agree to that, Lloyd?'

Lloyd stared grimly at Struan. 'I'm being railroaded,' he said heavily.

'Yes, you are,' Struan agreed. 'There should be more of it. Now, are you two going to agree or am I going to miss the birth of our baby? Well?'

Sally nodded slowly. A month's trial. A chance. 'I'd. . . I'd like that.'

'Lloyd?'

'I have no choice,' Lloyd said heavily. 'But if she turns out to be as irresponsible as I suspect——'

'Oh, for heaven's sake, man, go put your head in a bucket,' Struan snapped. 'Sally, welcome to the staff. Despite the great Lloyd Neale, I have a feeling you'll be happy here.'

CHAPTER TWO

WHEW. . .

Sally thumped her suitcases through the door of the hospital flat and surveyed her new home.

It was lovely. The apartment had been built at the rear of the hospital and its wide windows looked out to sea. She crossed to the living-room curtains and pulled them wide, then threw open the windows to let in the smell of the ocean.

Maybe this place could restore her delight in the world. The last few months had all but knocked the stuffing out of her—the months since her father's dreadful death and then the accusations and the recriminations. . .

The inquest had cleared her. It was only her head that made her keep reliving that dreadful night—asking herself over and over if there had been anything else that could have been done.

'Stop it, Sally,' she told herself aloud. 'It's over. Over. This place will be OK.'

It had to be OK. It had to be. Despite Lloyd Neale. . .

What was eating the man? Had he a permanent chip on his shoulder because of his injury? What on earth had happened to make him survey the world with such gloom?

It didn't matter. He had nothing to do with her. Somehow she would find a way to work with him, but his gloom needn't affect her.

It already had. Sally's joy at getting the job was overshadowed by Lloyd's disapproval. His look stayed with her. He had looked at her as if. . .

'As if I were a porriwiggle,' she said out loud, and a chuckle welled up inside as her humour reasserted itself. 'And a particularly irresponsible porriwiggle at that.'

'What's a porriwiggle?'

Sally jumped about a foot. She whirled around to find a solemn-faced child of about ten, ponytailed, freckled, and with one scratched knee, regarding her with interest.

'I. . .I beg you pardon?'

'What's a porriwiggle?' the little girl asked. She smiled shyly. 'Something to do with porridge?'

Sally smiled. 'I shouldn't think so,' she said cautiously. 'I think it's a bit like a tadpole. It was what my father called me whenever I was being obnoxious.'

'Obnoxious.' The child rolled the word around her tongue with satisfaction. 'An obnoxious porriwiggle. Is that what you are?'

The chuckle surfaced deliciously, driving away the unpleasant taste of Lloyd Neale. 'I hope not.'

Sally studied the little girl, covertly noting her school uniform and the tearstains on rather grubby cheeks. She held out her hand.

'Hi. I'm Sally Atchinson. I've just come to work here, and they tell me this is my new home.' She met the child's blank look. 'That is, unless it's already taken?' Her eyebrows lifted in polite enquiry.

'Oh, no. . .' The child gulped. 'I mean. . .' She took a deep breath and held out her hand to take Sally's. 'I'm Lisa. I don't live here any more.'

'But you used to?'

'Yes. Before Gina and Dad got married.'

Gina and Dad. . . Sally nodded thoughtfully. 'So you're. . .' She ventured a wild guess. There couldn't be many Ginas in such a small town. 'You're Dr Maitland's daughter?'

'Well, not really,' Lisa said truthfully. 'My mum died

when I was five, and Gina and Dad adopted me. I can't remember my own father so I call Dad Dad, but I remember my mum so I call Gina Gina.'

'Clear as mud,' Sally said roundly.

The child gave a rather watery giggle. She looked over at Sally's suitcases. 'You. . . You must be the new surgeon, then.'

'I am.'

Lisa nodded. 'I thought you must be. I knew you were being interviewed this morning.' She looked up at Sally and swallowed. 'I hope. . .I hope you don't mind me being in your flat.'

'Oh, no,' Sally told her, her eyes still on the child's tearstains. 'It would have been lonely if you hadn't been here to welcome me.' She glanced at her watch. 'Something tells me, though, Lisa, that at two o'clock on a Wednesday afternoon you should be in school.'

'Oh, yeah. . .' Lisa swallowed again. 'The fact is,' she whispered, 'I'm hiding.'

'You're hiding?'

'I left school at lunchtime,' Lisa said desperately. 'And the girls in the kitchen said Gina was having the baby and couldn't see me. So I went looking for Dad, and I knew he'd be in the labour ward with Gina, but when I got there I heard Gina crying. She was crying as if it really hurt. And the nurse came out and said I couldn't go in, and she said I should go back to school and not worry, but I can't.' She gulped. 'I just can't.'

'Oh, of course you can't.' Sally sank down on to the wide settee and gathered the tearstained poppet to her. 'Of course you can't, Lisa. Not with amazing family events taking place right here.' She fished in her skirt pocket for a handkerchief and wiped Lisa's cheeks and nose, and then held the child closer. 'Am I right in thinking you might be a bit scared?'

'Just a bit,' the child confessed. She gulped. 'In fact. . . In fact, a lot.'

'Your dad should have come out to see you.' Sally frowned. 'Does he know you're here?'

'Well. . .'

Sally fixed her with a look. 'Well, what, young lady?' Her voice was stern, but she smiled down at the child with understanding. The tearstained child met her look and tried a smile in return.

'Well, I don't usually come home from school at lunchtime. I'm not supposed to. But. . . But Gina was really quiet at breakfast, and I just knew something was going to happen. So I came.' She gulped. 'Sally, Gina sounds. . . She sounds as if it's really hurting. And my mum. . . My mum died. You don't think. . . You don't think my Gina's going to die too, do you?'

Sally's smile faded at the terror behind the hesitant whisper. 'No, I don't,' Sally said firmly. 'I very definitely do not think she is going to die. It seems to me that your Gina is a very normal young mum about to deliver a very normal new baby. Mums do it all the time. As well as that, she has Dr Maine and your dad looking after her every minute while your new little one is being born.'

'But. . . But she's crying.'

'And I don't blame her,' Sally said soundly. 'The thing is, young Lisa, that having a baby can be a very uncomfortable experience. And sometimes, when ladies are very, very uncomfortable, they yell. I would myself, I think. It's one time when ladies are allowed to let their hair down and yell their lungs out if they want to.'

'Really?' Lisa's eyes were huge. 'Wh—why?'

'Well. . .' Sally took a deep breath. Goodness, she was getting herself into hot water in this job. This couldn't be helped, though. One scared child needed to be reassured, and reassured fast.

'I haven't had a baby myself, of course,' Sally

continued gamely, 'so I'm going on what I've been told, and what I've seen when I've helped deliver babies. But my cousin had a fat, healthy baby last year and she told me that having a baby feels like pushing out a big, slippery pumpkin.'

'Pushing out. . .' Lisa's eyes nearly started out of her head. 'You mean. . . You mean like pooing?'

'It's not quite the same process.' Sally fought to keep her voice steady and failed in the attempt. 'But. . . But I gather the feeling's the same.'

'Pooing a pumpkin. . . Oooh. Ouch!'

'Exactly,' Sally said, still fighting laughter. 'There's nothing dangerous involved. Just lots of pushing and stretching and very, very hard work. So, if Gina wants to yell while this pumpkin's being born, then I don't think anyone should stop her, do you?'

'N-no. . .' Lisa was impressed. She shook her head. 'I don't blame her. No wonder. . .'

Sally chuckled. She stood up, holding her hand out for the child to take. 'I think we should go back to the labour ward and find out exactly what's happening, don't you, Lisa, instead of hiding here in my flat? The chances are if Gina's making a lot of noise then this baby's just about out.'

'This pumpkin, you mean,' Lisa giggled. The toilet humour of a ten-year-old was entranced. Her fears put aside, the little girl took Sally's hand and started towards the door. 'Actually,' she confessed, 'that's just the shape it looked inside Gina. I hope it doesn't look like one when it gets out.'

The labour ward was at the other end of the hospital. As Sally and Lisa approached, they could hear clearly that labour was very much at end-stage. The room wasn't soundproofed and Gina was consecutively swearing and puffing. The sounds echoed down the corridor towards them and Sally looked down at Lisa in concern. Maybe she should keep the child away.

Lisa, though, was not worrying. Now that the process had been explained to her satisfaction, she was entranced.

'Wow!' she whispered. 'It does sound like hard work. She sounds like she's pushing a steamroller. Why do ladies have babies if they hurt so much?'

'Well, I guess they think they're worth it.' Sally smiled. 'A few hours' solid effort and they have a scamp like you to cope with for the rest of their lives. Now, let's find someone who can tell us what's going on.'

There was no nurse in sight and the corridor was deserted. Sally hesitated. She wanted a nurse to appear, but if Gina was close to delivery they'd be occupied. She looked uncertainly down at Lisa. 'I don't think we ought to knock,' she told the child. 'What say we sit here in the waiting-room and wait?'

'And listen,' Lisa breathed. 'I didn't think Gina knew words like that.'

Sally grinned. 'She doesn't,' she told the child. 'Tomorrow Gina will forget she ever knew them and she won't remember saying them at all. You wait and see. And don't you dare tell her you heard her say them.'

'I won't.' Then the child swung around at the sound of halting footsteps behind them and her small face crinkled into a smile of welcome. 'Lloyd!'

Lloyd Neale. . . .

Oh, great. Here was the last person Sally wanted to see. Just the person to aid and abet a small child eavesdropping on the birth of her younger brother or sister. Sally gritted her teeth as she looked around at the physician's approach.

'Young Lisa.' The tall, white-coated doctor paused, his eyebrows creasing together in concern. 'What on earth are you doing here?' And then Lloyd's voice cut

off sharply as he realised whose hand Lisa was clutching. 'You——'

'Lloyd, this is Sally.' Lisa's tears were forgotten. The
child jumped to her feet and bounced forward to clutch
Lloyd's hand, oblivious of his grim stare. 'Sally's our
new surgeon, Lloyd.' Lisa smiled. 'She's really Dr
Atchinson, but she doesn't seem like a doctor to me.'

'Not like a doctor. . .?' Lloyd flicked Sally an
unreadable look as Lisa's hold on his hand tightened.

'No,' Lisa agreed. 'She says she's an obnoxious porriwiggle, but she doesn't seem like that either. I came
home at lunchtime because I was scared about Gina,
and I heard Gina yell and got even scareder, and I
went to hide in Sally's apartment so they couldn't send
me back to school, but Sally found me, and she told me
Gina's just yelling because babies feel like pumpkins.'

'Pumpkins. . .' Lloyd was clearly lost. 'Hey, Lisa,
slow down.'

'Well, they do,' Lisa said importantly. 'Having a
baby is like pooing a pumpkin—just as uncomfortable—and Sally says any lady doing it is allowed to
yell any way they want, and I'm not even allowed to
tell Gina tomorrow that she really knows all those bad
words. . .'

Lloyd stared down at the child clutching his hand.
His deep grey eyes creased in astonishment as his hand
came to rest on Lisa's shoulder.

Uh-oh. . . Sally thought. Of all the people to tell. . .

'A pumpkin. . .' he said blankly.

'Yeah, and it looked just like one when it was still
inside Gina,' Lisa told him. 'And at the end it was
almost as hard—only sometimes it wriggled and Gina
let me feel.' She winced as a low moan came through
the door. 'And that's why Gina's so uncomfortable
now, and Sally says the more Gina yells the closer it
is to coming out. She says Gina has to work really,
really hard—and that maybe we shouldn't knock.'

The moan from the labour ward died to nothing. There was absolute silence. Lloyd stared from the child to Sally and back to the child. Then, to Sally's amazement, the cold grey eyes lost their ice.

His lips twitched. Unsuspected laughter lines creased around Lloyd's eyes and his face transformed. The laughter lines deepened, until Sally was almost smiling back. She watched in disbelief as Lloyd's deep, rich laughter echoed down the corridor.

Was this really the same man? The cold-eyed, arrogant male she had tripped was gone. Instead, this laughing, white-coated doctor was stooping to give Lisa a hard hug, and the eyes that looked over the child's curls to Sally's apprehensive face were warm with appreciation.

'That's not what we tell the mothers in natural childbirth classes, Dr Atchinson.' Lloyd grinned. 'I've never heard pumpkins being so much as mentioned.'

Sally gave an uncertain smile. 'It seemed the best way. . .'

'To explain this.' He cast an expressive glance at the closed door and then hugged Lisa again. 'I couldn't agree more. Lisa, does your dad know you're here?'

'He thinks I'm at school.'

'Well, I think we have to let him know——' Then Lloyd's word were clipped off. A short, gasping cry, different from all the rest, came from within the labour ward, and then there were maybe five long seconds of silence. The small group in the corridor held their collective breath.

And then there was another cry which wasn't Gina's. It was a baby's cry.

Lisa turned as if struck, and stared straight at the door. The cry deepened, strengthening by the moment, as a new little person announced displeasure to the world at ejection from the world's most comfortable position.

'It's born,' Lisa whispered. 'I heard. . .I heard our baby being born.'

Lloyd's smile was still lighting his whole face. His grey eyes were glinting in laughter. His stick dropped to the floor and strong arms swung Lisa high above his head.

'You did that, young Lisa. You have a brother or sister.'

'Which?' Lisa swung wildly at full stretch of Lloyd's arms and laughed down at him, ponytail flying. 'Which is it?'

'I don't know,' Lloyd confessed.

'It'll be a boy if it's making all that fuss,' the child said scornfully. 'What's the bet?'

'I'm not betting.' Lloyd laughed. He set her down and flicked her wayward ponytail. 'I think we should go and find out.' He retrieved his stick, limped forward and knocked on the door.

A nurse opened it a crack, and when she saw who it was she opened it further. 'Oh, Dr Neale. She's just delivered. A fine baby——'

'Don't tell me,' Lloyd interrupted harshly, cutting her off mid-sentence. 'There's someone here who has the right to know before I do.' He gestured behind to where Lisa was staring, open-mouthed. 'Tell Struan and Gina that Lisa's out here, will you?'

'Sure.' The nurse cast an uncertain glance at the child she had told to return to school an hour before, and disappeared into the room. Ten seconds later a beaming, exuberant Struan Maitland swept out to lift Lisa high and hug her hard.

'Lisa. . . What the heck. . .? We thought you were at school, sweetheart,' he told his daughter. 'I was just going to come and get you.'

'You were?'

'Sure was.' Struan's hold tightened. 'As soon as this baby was born, I was going to walk right into your classroom and say, "Could I take my daughter home, please? Because she is required to meet her brand new"——'

'Pumpkin,' Lisa squealed. 'I have to meet my pumpkin. Is he really here?'

'Pumpkin.' Struan looked bemused. 'Lisa, actually we thought we might call her Sarah, but if you have your heart set on "Pumpkin". . .'

'A girl. . .' Lisa gave a crow of delight and wriggled down. Grabbing her father's hand she tugged hard. 'Can I see?'

'Of course.' The proud father led her towards the door and then paused to look back at Lloyd and Sally.

'I'm not sure what's been going on out here,' he said slowly, 'but I think I might have cause to be grateful to you two.'

'Not me.' Lloyd grinned. 'It's our new surgeon who's been imparting the facts of life to your daughter. I told you you might regret this appointment, Struan.' Lloyd's smile didn't slip, though, and the laughing eyes he turned on Sally were warm with humour.

Deep inside, Sally felt a stirring of the embryo feeling that had been embedded the first time she had seen this man. She didn't know what it was. All she knew was that it was there, it was disturbing, and it was starting to grow.

Struan's eyes went from one to the other, but too much had happened in too short a time for him to take it all in. His daughter tugged his hand and he shrugged and turned away. 'OK, Lisa. Let's go and meet Pumpkin.'

Lisa nodded. 'Lloyd, you look after Sally,' she ordered seriously. 'She's only just arrived.' She smiled shyly up at Sally. 'Thanks, Sally,' she smiled. And she disappeared.

'Oh, Gina,' they heard the little girl whisper as the

door started to close behind her. 'Oh, Gina, isn't she red?'

Lloyd and Sally were left standing in the deserted corridor. The sounds within the labour ward muted to a delighted murmur as Sally's smile slowly slipped away. It had been great for a moment. Hostilities forgotten. . .

It seemed the truce wasn't completely over. Lloyd stood looking uncertainly down at her, but then his smile returned once again to his face. Once more that heart-stopping smile.

'Dr Atchinson. . .' He grimaced, but the smile didn't leave his eyes. 'I think. . . If Lisa's ordered me to look after you, then maybe we might start by burying the hatchet.'

Sally stared up at him, no answering smile in her eyes. Her heart was doing strange things. 'What. . . what do you mean?'

'Well,' he started, 'We've agreed to a month's trial. I know we can't work together if we've agreed to hate each other. So. . . So let's call a truce. You've been very kind to a child who means a lot to me. So maybe. . .'

'So maybe I'm not all bad?'

He nodded, his eyes impassive. 'So maybe you're not all bad.'

'Just impetuous and irresponsible?'

His look didn't change. 'Tell you what. Let's just leave it as impetuous.'

'The minor crime?'

'The minor crime.' He nodded.

Sally nodded slowly. 'Then, instead of convicting you of being an arrogant bore, I could just sentence you for suffering wounded pride.'

His look did change, then. They stood, staring at each other for a long, long moment. Was his temper going to explode again? Sally wondered, and found herself almost waiting for it. It wasn't to happen, though. Finally, finally the trace of laughter came back into Lloyd's eyes. Heaven knew what effort it cost to put it there.

'Granted,' he said softly, and held out his hand.

Sally took it. Her fingers were clasped in a grip of steel. His hand held her and warmed her, and the strange stirrings inside became a hollow ache.

What on earth is wrong with me? she asked herself crossly as she avoided those piercing grey eyes and gave herself a mental shake.

She was hungry. That was what the matter was. She'd had one biscuit since the night before. She pulled her hand from Lloyd's grip and managed a half-hearted smile.

'If we really are at peace, maybe you could show me where I can eat,' she suggested, trying to keep her voice firm.

He frowned. 'No one's offered you lunch?'

Sally shook her head. 'I gather things are confused— what with Gina and Struan and Lesley being so occupied. I took a quick walk around the hospital and one of the nurses showed me the flat at the rear—but then I found Lisa.'

He nodded. 'So you haven't had anything since breakfast?'

'Since last night,' she told him. 'I was running late this morning. I thought I'd stop along the way for breakfast but I had a flat tyre and then I met some cows.'

'Welcome to the country, Dr Atchinson.' He smiled and glanced at his watch. 'Tell you what. I have half an hour free now. I was supposed to be doing an anaesthetic for Struan while he operated on a hernia, but he's otherwise occupied. The nurses have tucked Mr Hammer back into bed and told him he'll be waiting until tomorrow.'

Sally looked up, startled. 'I could do it,' she told him. 'If it's urgent. . .'

'It's not,' he promised. 'It's not strangulating, and it's too late to change our minds now. Mr Hammer was delighted to know the operation was to be delayed and tucked into a big roast lunch as soon as he heard. So that's on the list for tomorrow. And Struan will be delighted that you're doing it and not him. So. . . The kitchen staff are off duty now, and won't be back until four, but I have a refrigerator full of eggs, courtesy of a grateful patient with too many chooks, and I'm a dab hand at an omelette. So you have an invitation, Dr Atchinson.'

Sally stared up at him, her eyes troubled, and Lloyd shrugged.

'I know. . .' He spread his hands. 'OK, this might even be construed as an olive-branch.' He reached out to touch her hand lightly. 'The truth is, Dr Atchinson, that I reacted badly to being knocked down. My recovery's been a slow and painful business and I'm always expecting a relapse. So. . . So for a moment I was scared that I'd damaged something, and I took that fear out on you. Now, will that do as an apology?'

Sally's stare widened. She didn't believe it. The man was apologising. Already. . .

She made herself smile. For the life of her she couldn't think what else to do.

'That's very generous of you,' she said slowly. 'Especially since I was negligent.' She met his look and took a deep breath. 'And it's true—I could have hurt you. I'm so grateful that I didn't.'

'Well, that makes two of us.' The laughter was back behind his smile again and the knot was back in Sally's stomach. 'So, does that mean I'm making an omelette?'

'Yes, please.' Sally smiled shyly up at him. 'That would be lovely.'

*   *   *

Like Sally's, Lloyd's apartment was attached to the hospital, but his was at the other end, close to the labour ward. It also looked out over the sea, and was a mirror image of Sally's. Unlike Sally's spartan apartment, with its unpacked suitcases and pristine, unused look, Lloyd's flat looked as though it had been lived in for years. Sally stared around at the comfortable muddled appearance and said as much.

'I've been here for years, off and on,' Lloyd told her. 'I started training as an anaesthetist, got fed up with it, and came here as a family medicine trainee. The place hooked me. I had another stint in the city while I did my physician training, but I always intended coming back—so my stuff was stored.' He grinned. 'They reckoned it was good collateral—holding my music collection until I came back.'

Sally walked over to the piles of compact discs strewn over the desk.

'Hey. . . Every Beatles album ever released, re-released on CDs. I'm jealous!'

Lloyd was in the kitchenette at the other end of the room. He lifted a carton of eggs from the refrigerator and put them on the bench.

'If you're good I'll give them to you as a wedding-present.'

Sally stared. 'I. . .I beg your pardon? I'm not getting married.'

'No.' Lloyd's stick was leaning by the wall—he could obviously manage without it when the need arose. Now he cracked and separated the eggs expertly. 'But I am. And Margaret—my fiancée—can't stand the Beatles. Her taste is purely classical. I might keep one or two, but it's no use keeping the whole collection.'

Sally stared. To go without the Beatles. . .'That's some sacrifice,' she told him.

'It is, isn't it?'

'How can you marry someone who doesn't share

your music tastes?' Sally asked slowly. 'I think I'd
go mad.'

'Maybe there are more important things in life
than music?'

'I guess,' Sally said cautiously. 'Like sharing a sense
of the ridiculous or. . .'

'Or a sense of responsibility,' Lloyd finished for her.
'How hungry are you?'

'Starving,' she confessed, and he smiled and cracked
a third egg.

'An appreciative victim. Well, well. . .' Deftly he
whipped the whites to a light white froth, folded in
herbs and yolks and poured all into a waiting pan. 'So
tell me, Dr Atchinson. . . Or Miss Atchinson, if you're
a surgeon. . .'

'Doctor's fine.' Sally smiled, grinning at the inherent
silliness of medical labelling, dating back to when
surgeons had been the town barbers. 'Or Sally's even
better.'

'So tell me, Sally.' Lloyd smiled back as the omelette
sizzled in the pan. 'What's a just-qualified surgeon—
I refuse to believe you qualified any further back than
last week—doing applying for a job in Gundowring?'

'That's easy. The sea and the weather.'

His smile faded a little. 'And that's all?'

'No.' She shook her head as she silently thought.
'Of course it isn't. I just. . .I was just tired of hospital
queues and only getting to see my patients for ten
minutes post-op. I've done most of my training in a
big public hospital. Interviews and examinations were
done by residents. It was my job to check the diagnosis
was correct and perform the operation. I hardly talked
to a patient. In the end I was beginning to feel like a
technician—not a doctor.'

'Like me and anaesthetics.' He nodded. 'So you
came to the country?'

'So I came to the country.' Sally looked appreciatively down at the crisp, golden omelette Lloyd was lifting on to a plate. Her mouth almost watered. She sank down at the table as Lloyd limped around to put it before her. 'Yum!'

'My favourite compliment,' he smiled. 'Yum. Wine?'

'No, thank you.' She glanced up at him and smiled back into those penetrating eyes. 'I'd fall asleep all over your omelette.'

He poured fruit juice, and then came to sit beside her as she ate. 'Go on. Eat. I ate at a civilised hour.'

Despite her hunger, Sally found it hard to concentrate on her food with Lloyd Neale watching her as she ate. His calm grey eyes rested on her thoughtfully, as if he was trying to work out the answer to an enigma. They didn't talk. The silence wasn't uncomfortable— but it was disturbing, none the less.

The man was so darned compelling. A magnetic personality. She'd heard the term before, but until now hadn't known what it meant. Think about omelette, Sally told herself fiercely as she forced another mouthful down. And don't think about those eyes.

Impossible!

Finally she finished. She rose and carried her plate to the sink.

'Don't touch the dishes,' Lloyd ordered, and Sally raised her eyebrows at him.

'I don't believe it. A man who not only cooks, but washes dishes! Where have you been all my life?'

'I'm claimed,' he smiled, and Sally smiled sardonically back.

'Lucky Margaret.'

He had the grace to grimace and shake his head. 'Well, in fact, Mrs Knowles cleans up for me. If I leave the dishes on the sink they magically get done.'

'And honest!' Sally smiled.

'Mrs Knowles will look after you too,' Lloyd told her, meeting her smile. 'Once you get started here you'll need her. You're going to be busy. Most of our general surgery has had to go to Melbourne while we've been without a general surgeon, but there's heaps of it to be done, and the better you are, the more there'll be for you to do.'

'So, should I behave incompetently?'

'Pick your mark,' he told her. 'Lorna Dalziel is our resident Munchausen's case. With her I'd act as incompetent as you possibly can. One scrap of sympathy and you'll be seeing her every other day.'

Munchausen's. . . The compulsive imagining of medical disorders. Sally grimaced. There was one in every medical practice, it seemed. 'Lorna Dalziel,' she murmured, committing the name to memory. 'Thanks for the warning.'

'Any time,' he said lightly. 'Lorna spends her mornings in our waiting-rooms and her afternoons in the vet's waiting-room, trying to get her dogs treated for all sorts of weird and wonderful complaints. Now, you said you'd seen round the hospital. Have you checked out the theatre?'

'The charge sister showed me. It looks well set up.'

'It's our boast that this is the best equipped country hospital this side of Melbourne. Gundowring has really grown as a medical centre in the past few years, and we're proud of it. Would you like to see your consulting-room?'

'I would.' Sally hesitated. 'If you have time to show me.'

He glanced at his watch. 'The consulting-rooms are in a suite at the front. I have patients booked in fifteen minutes. I could walk you over and you can come back by yourself?'

'Sound fine by me.' Sally waited until he'd retrieved his stick. She walked to the door and opened it, then stood aside to let Lloyd pass.

It was a mistake. He frowned and took the door-handle from her. 'After you,' he snapped.

Sally moistened her lips. The man was so darned sensitive.

'You know, that doesn't make sense,' she ventured as she walked out before him. 'Walking-stick or no walking-stick, I was being nice to someone who's just fed me. Are you trying to make me feel bad for being considerate?'

His brows snapped together and his lips tightened. 'If you like.'

'Why?'

He stopped then, and turned to face her. They'd reached the path running round the side of the hospital. The warm sea air blew softly between them, diffusing the static of anger.

'I don't like being made to feel a cripple,' he snapped.

Sally took a deep breath. Whew. . .

So now what? Should she say nothing, as befitted junior surgeon ticked off by senior physician, or should she venture forth where angels feared to tread? No choice, really. Being told off without justification wasn't Sally's style.

'But. . . But you're not a cripple,' she said softly. 'You just walk with a limp.'

'Butt out, Dr Atchinson.'

Sally frowned. 'I'm sorry. . .I didn't mean to be rude.' They moved off together down the path and Sally looked down at his foot. It was dragging a little.

If she didn't say something now she'd have to look the other way every time he limped. For heaven's sake, the man was making a mountain out of a molehill.

'I guess it has to be spinal damage,' she said slowly, thinking aloud. 'Sciatica? Surely not. Dr Maitland said you'd had an accident. What sort of accident?'

It was as if she was standing on raw nerves. 'Do you always shove your nose in where it's least wanted?'

Sally grimaced, and then smiled apologetically up at him. 'I'm sorry,' she repeated. 'My father says——' She caught herself on a sharp jab of pain and corrected herself. 'My father *said* it's my least appealing characteristic. My nosiness, he called it. It's an annoying trait that I try to curb.' She ventured another smile up at his hostile face. 'The thing is, if you're working with me as anaesthetist then I really need to know your physical capabilities.'

He didn't smile back. Anger was overwhelming. 'I can stand as long as you can,' he snapped. 'And that's all you need to know.'

'But you'd rather I didn't schedule long sessions? It's OK with me. I could split operating sessions into two short ones per day instead of one long——'

'I told you, Dr Atchinson, I don't want any consideration.' His eyes were snapping black with anger. 'Especially from you.'

End of conversation.

Sally walked silently on, her mind working at a hundred miles an hour. This man. . . He was a chameleon, capable of warmth and laughter, and tied to pride and ruthless coldness.

Why, for heaven's sake? What on earth had happened to the man to make him feel like this?

And why do you need to know? she asked herself as they neared the glass doors leading to the consulting-rooms. Sure, Lloyd Neale has a chip on his shoulder, but it shouldn't be important to you, Sally Atchinson. He's a happily engaged man. . .

Not happily.

You don't know that.

'Dr Neale. . .'

An urgent female voice stopped Sally's thoughts in their tracks. Sally looked over to the main entrance to the hospital, where a uniformed nurse was hurrying towards them. 'Oh, thank heaven,' the nurse gasped as she reached them. 'I thought you must have gone into town.'

'What is it, May?' Lloyd demanded.

'We've a burn case coming in,' the nurse told him. 'It sounds nasty. The council road workers have been filling pot-holes just out of town—moving from hole to hole with a tub of wet tar, which they left on the truck tray between holes. One of the men slipped from the back of the truck and the hot tar went with him. The men say his face is coated in it. They've radioed to say they're bringing him in now.'

Lloyd nodded. 'I'll come now. How long before they arrive?'

'It will be any minute.' The nurse looked uncertainly to Sally. 'Should I. . .? Should I ask Dr Maitland to come? I know he's with his wife and their new baby. . .'

'I'll assist,' Sally said firmly. 'There's no need to disturb Dr Maitland.'

Lloyd flashed her a long, searching look and finally nodded.

'OK, Dr Atchinson,' he snapped. 'Your first emergency. Let's see what you're made of.'

CHAPTER THREE

THE nurse's face cleared and she turned back to Casualty, Lloyd and Sally with her. Lloyd wasn't slowed by his limp, Sally noticed. When he needed to he could move so fast that Sally and the nurse were both struggling to keep up.

They got to the casualty entrance just as a council road-truck pulled up. The passenger door swung open and a man emerged, pausing to half pull, half lift the man sitting beside him down on to the driveway.

Sally's eyes widened with horror.

Hot tar. . .

The man's head was unrecognisable under a thick mat of black resin, glued in an impermeable mass from the top of his head down to a thick coating across his shoulders. How on earth could he be breathing?

It seemed he was. The man's feet were still supporting him, even moving unsteadily forward as the driver came around and took his other shoulder, the two workers bringing their mate forward for help.

The nurse was standing at the door to Casualty, gazing in stupefaction at the injured man. Lloyd brushed past her.

'Who is it?' he demanded of the man's friends.

'Henry. . . Henry Butler.'

'Right, Henry. Let's get you out of trouble.' Lloyd moved to the man's side, edging one of the friends aside, and Sally noted his strength as he took over the support of the injured Henry. 'Get a trolley,' he ordered, and then his voice hardened in urgency. 'Sister, get a trolley.'

'Oh. . . Of course. . .' The nurse jerked to her

senses and turned to shift a trolley into position. As she did, the injured man's legs buckled under him and he gave a strangling, choking moan.

'Lift!' Lloyd's voice was urgent. The man's mate stared helplessly down at his crumpled friend. Before the full weight of the man was taken by Lloyd, Sally was there, taking his side.

They moved as one, driven by urgency. Both could see that the man's airway had blocked. They had no time at all. . .

Lloyd didn't have to speak. Sally lifted with him, her slight weight moving in a professional lift. Together they hauled the man up on to the trolley, rolling him on his side.

His airway. . . Sally's fingers were in the man's mouth almost before the side of his face made contact with the trolley, and what she felt made her wince. A mat of warm, sticky tar. . .

She crouched beside him, her fingers working to get the sticky stuff out of his throat. It stuck to her fingers. She brought her hand out, wiped the stuff off and inserted her hand again.

'A tube,' she snapped.

Lloyd was already moving. He'd looked down and seen she was in control, and Sally's fingers were better than his at trying to re-establish an airway.

'Resus trolley,' he snapped. 'Fast!'

The man's mates were standing back, appalled.

'He was OK,' one of them whispered. 'I thought. . .I thought he was just burned.'

Lloyd had wheeled around to the switch beside the door. He hit it three times hard—three hard rings. Sally counted in her head as she fought for space in the back of the man's throat. Five seconds. . . Six. . .

She couldn't insert an endotracheal tube without the resus trolley. For heaven's sake, where was it?

Matron, a senior nurse and the scared junior with

the crash cart arrived at the same moment.

'Tracheotomy?' Lloyd snapped. If they couldn't get air through the man's mouth they would have to cut.

'I don't think I can. . .' Sally stared helplessly down at the man's neck. It was a mat of tar. How could she cut her way fast through that lot? 'I doubt. . .' Her fingers moved in the man's mouth, she shifted them and a thick clot of tar came with them. The man's chest heaved and a whistling, searing breath of air went in.

'Right.' Sally shoved her cleaner hand in. 'Tube. Now. . .' She had it clear. If she could get a tube in to establish a clear airway. . .

Lloyd was already moving in, endotracheal tube in his hand. Sally tilted the man's mouth so that she lifted his jaw forward, her fingers cleared the muck once again and she signalled to Lloyd. His anaesthetic training came to the fore. He moved swiftly into position behind the man's head, the laryngoscope slid down the man's throat within seconds, and the tube slid safely into place.

They were lucky. The man's unconsciousness lifted almost immediately. He fought his way into wakefulness, thrashing against their hands at the feel of the tube. Sally held his arms and signalled Matron to do the same.

'Let's get a sedative in fast,' Lloyd said. 'And a relaxant. I think we'll breathe him for a while.' He turned to the trolley, searching for what he wanted, while Sally's grip on the man's hand tightened.

He was frantic—way out of control. Burned and now this. . .

'Henry, don't fight us,' Sally told him. 'We've put a tube in to help you breathe. We'll get you pain-free in a moment. Try and help us. Try not to fight.'

Amazingly the man heard. He slumped back, and Lloyd swiftly inserted the syringe.

Once again Sally counted, but she did so while she assessed the situation. Ten. . . Eleven. . . Then the relaxant took hold. She felt the tension go out of him and Lloyd took over bag-breathing.

Now. . .

'Let's get the heat out of the tar,' Lloyd said grimly. 'It'll still be burning under there.'

He was right. Sally put her hand on the man's head and winced.

'We'll move him into Theatre.' She cast a sympathetic glance at the man's two mates. 'We've got him breathing again,' she told them. 'Sister will take you through to the waiting-room and take particulars.' She nodded to the junior nurse and then turned to Matron. 'Let's get hoses linked to the sink in Theatre. Now!'

The stuff steamed for nearly ten minutes as they washed more and more water over it. Lloyd was fully occupied with breathing for the injured man. It was up to Sally to do the rest—carefully protecting the tubing as she worked, but thoroughly cooling every section. Every time she let herself relax for a moment, the horror of what was happening washed over her with the water. She thought of the damage that was going on beneath the tar. Heaven alone knew. . .

Had he got his eyes closed before the stuff hit? Sally turned the man's face slightly, so the water poured down over his gummed-up eyes. If he wasn't to lose all hope of sight, they had to stop the burning.

The entire team was soaked, and the floor of Theatre was awash. There would be time for mopping up afterwards.

There was sobbing out in the corridor. Someone must have brought in the man's wife, and Lloyd sent one of the nurses out to see.

'Do you want her to come in?' the young nurse quavered, and Lloyd shook his head.

'Get her a cup of tea. One look at her husband like this and we'll have two patients on our hands.'

Finally Sally was satisfied that the heat was gone. She stood back from the table and looked down at her patient. Now what?

'We need to send him to Melbourne,' she said slowly. That was where she wanted him to be—somewhere with the world's finest plastic surgeons, who would know just what to do. And a first class ophthalmologist. . .

'It will have to wait until morning.' Lloyd looked at the monitors and noted their satisfactory message. 'I know the air ambulance has been called already for a three-car smash further north. What do you think about the tar?'

'There's no heat left in it now,' Sally said cautiously. 'But. . .'

'But?'

'But I'm darned if I'll try to take it off.' Sally grimaced. 'It can stay just where it is.'

'For how long?' Lloyd was frowning.

'I'm not sure. But. . .' Sally thought back to a patient's tar-coated hand she had seen during training. The plastic surgeon had been adamant.

'We can get it off by mixing peanut oil and kerosene,' she said slowly. 'But it's a painful business, and skin tends to stick fast to the tar. A partial thickness burn will turn to a full thickness one if we're not careful. And, in fact, it may be better to leave the tar where it is anyway. It's a sterile dressing in itself.'

'You've seen this before?'

'Only on a hand,' Sally confessed.

'What about the eyes?'

Sally bit her lip. 'If his eyes were open when the tar

hit, then the damage must be already done. The eyes wouldn't take that sort of heat without irreparable damage.' She fingered the set tar around Henry's eyelids. 'But by the shape of this. . . It hasn't been disturbed, and if his eyes were open then his eyelids would have shifted the stuff before it set, and you'd have wedges of tar shoved downwards—I'm willing to bet the lids are closed. And in that case. . . In that case, then they're also better left until it can be removed under the care of an ophthalmologist.'

'You mean, we send him to Melbourne, tar intact?' The physician in Lloyd was appalled. 'You're kidding.'

'It's the safest.'

He stared across the table at her. 'It's rare for a surgeon to opt for the non-procedural route.'

'Too rare,' Sally agreed, knowing a number of her colleagues would have been aching to get in and clear off the tar. 'But honestly, Lloyd, the skin will slough this off itself soon enough—with a bit of gentle help. And I don't want full thickness burns.'

'They might be already there.'

'In which case they'll weep, and the tar will slough off all the faster. Or he'll infect and we'll have to go in. But for now—we wait and see.'

'Whew. . .' Lloyd was watching her strangely. 'Will you tell his wife?'

Sally frowned. Lloyd knew the man. It would be much better if he did the talking. Still. . . If he didn't want to. . . She squared her shoulders. 'Of course.'

'Even though I know Henry and his wife?'

Sally flushed. So she was being tested. She glared across at Lloyd. 'It's your role if you know them,' she said softly. 'But if you're reluctant, then it'll show. It's better that I do it.'

He held up his hands in appeasement, a tired smile lighting the back of his eyes.

'OK, Dr Atchinson. I agree. It's my role to speak to family.' His hand was lying on Henry's wrist and his eyes swung down to the burnt, tar-covered face. Henry was solidly unconscious now—free, for the time being, from pain. 'OK, Henry, let's take you through to the ward.'

Half an hour later they had Henry settled in Intensive Care. The breathing tube was still in place and would be at least until morning.

'There may be oedema if his throat has burned,' Sally decided. 'If there's swelling then the tube will have to stay in place for days. Even if there's not. . . The tar around his mouth is still soft. All he had to do is breathe some of that in. . .'

'The tube stays in place,' Lloyd agreed. 'Respirator tonight and we'll assess him in the morning.'

One nurse would be with him all the time, and would stay with him while he was on the respirator, but Lloyd and Sally were free to go. They walked out of the intensive care ward together.

'You know,' Lloyd said conversationally as the ward door closed behind them, 'I could get used to working with you, Dr Atchinson.'

Ditto for you, Sally thought, but she didn't return the compliment. After all, she had never cast doubts on Lloyd's ability as a doctor.

Even so, the thought stayed solidly in her mind. Lloyd Neale was a fine doctor. She'd liked the way he had treated Mrs Butler too. He'd spoken honestly and clearly, giving her the full picture without frightening her, laying open the possible complications but at the same time imparting reassurance.

Sounded easy, but Sally knew just how hard it was to do and do well.

'So much for my consultations,' Lloyd was saying ruefully. He glanced at his watch. 'It's almost dinner-time. I hope my receptionist has rescheduled them and they're not still waiting.'

'Lloyd!'

A woman's voice called from behind them and Lloyd stopped. Sally paused and glanced back.

The woman coming along the corridor was in her early thirties, Sally guessed. She could even have been younger, but the clothes she wore were plain and severe. They consisted of a sensible grey skirt and a quality white blouse. One gold brooch at her throat was her only adornment. She was tall and thin, with brown hair caught up in a tight French roll—the sort of hairstyle that took two hours to achieve on Sunday evening and then wasn't touched for a week. It looked as if it would crack if touched. Still, underneath the severity, the woman was quite attractive.

'Have you heard the news?' the woman was asking Lloyd. 'Struan and Gina had their baby. Isn't that lovely?'

'Lovely,' Lloyd agreed, the smile lighting his eyes in welcome. 'Margaret, this is Sally Atchinson, our new surgeon. Sally, Margaret Howard is our hospital administrator. And my fiancée.'

'Hi.' Sally put out a hand and was given a limp one to shake. The woman inspected her carefully, as if she were a rather interesting specimen of something distasteful.

'You don't look like a surgeon.' She placed a careful smile on her lips and turned back to Lloyd. 'I thought surgeons had to do years of training.'

'According to Sally, she's done them.' Lloyd's initial anger at Sally was obviously put aside for the moment. She'd been good, Sally thought irrepressibly, and gave herself a mental shake. 'She's here for a month's trial,' Lloyd continued.

'Oh. . .' The woman didn't say it, but the relief was obvious on her face. A month's trial was better than a permanent appointment. To her annoyance, Sally found herself flushing as the beginnings of anger stirred. 'Well, that's nice.' Another bright smile at Sally and then Margaret turned slightly, edging Sally out of the conversation in one almost imperceptible movement. 'Lloyd, Lisa is in with Gina and the new baby. I thought Gina and Struan might prefer to be alone tonight with their baby—so I wondered if I should offer to have Lisa.'

'I think Struan will want Lisa with them,' Lloyd said shortly, and Sally smiled inwardly. So, Margaret wasn't exempt from Lloyd's coldness.

'But they have their own child now. I mean. . . Well, I know they love Lisa—they've been so good to her— but she is adopted. . .'

Ugh. Sally's fingers curled in distaste.

'I doubt they'll love Lisa any less because of the new baby,' Lloyd said shortly. 'But by all means offer.'

'It'll mean we won't be able to go out.'

'Are we going out?' Lloyd asked.

'You haven't forgotten the concert?' Margaret raised her brows in gentle reproof. 'There's a quartet coming all the way from Sydney. But, Lloyd, it's chamber music. There's nothing worse than a child coughing and twitching and wanting to unwrap sticky sweets in the middle of quality music. We couldn't take her.'

'Of course you couldn't,' Sally agreed cordially, her fingers uncurling and the corners of her mouth twitching in the beginnings of laughter. She turned shocked eyes on Lloyd. 'How could you have thought it, Dr Neale? People have been run out of town for less.'

Lloyd met her look. To her surprise his eyes flashed a hint of responsive laughter, swiftly suppressed.

'Then we'll have to cancel the concert, Margaret. In

fact, I'm not happy about leaving Intensive Care.'

'Well, that's settled, then,' Margaret agreed. 'It's the only charitable thing to do, after all. But the cost is thirty dollars apiece, Lloyd. Do you suppose we can get a refund?'

'I'll buy them from you.' The idea sprang into Sally's head and she spoke without thinking. It was a good idea, though. Her lips twitched as Lloyd and Margaret turned to stare at her.

'You. . .' Margaret was clearly taken aback. 'But you don't like chamber music.'

'How on earth do you know that?' Sally smiled. Her eyes creased at Margaret's look of disapproval. Clearly the lady had done a lightening assessment and found her wanting. 'After heavy metal, it's my favourite,' she couldn't resist adding. 'And I have a quiet evening ahead. I'll enjoy it.'

'But you don't want both tickets. . .'

'Yes, I do.' Sally smiled. 'I'll find someone to come with me, even if it means wandering through the nursing home and offering. Honest. Give me the tickets, Margaret, and then go and do your Christian duty by Lisa.'

Margaret was already fishing in her bag.

'Are you sure?' Lloyd demanded suspiciously, and Sally raised her eyebrows at him.

'What's the matter, Dr Neale? Don't you think I'll pay for them?'

'I haven't a clue,' Lloyd said angrily. 'Margaret, we don't even know if you're looking after Lisa yet. If you're not, then you and Sally could go together.'

'Oh, I'm sure I will be,' Margaret said easily. 'They won't want Lisa. And sixty dollars, Lloyd. When we're saving so hard for a house and we've decided to increase your superannuation. . .I'm not looking a gift-horse in the mouth.'

'Thanks very much,' Sally said drily. She took the

proffered tickets and pocketed them. 'So I've stopped
being criminally negligent only to become a
gift-horse. . . Your opinion of me is going up by the
minute, Dr Neale.'

CHAPTER FOUR

SALLY spent the remainder of the evening unpacking
and setting herself up in her consulting-room. She grew
happier as she worked, stopping continually to look
out at the beckoning sea. The sun was sinking over
the distant hills, and the last crimson sheen was
reflecting in the smooth roll of the surf.

'You're all mine,' she whispered, as if such owner-
ship were possible. 'I'm employed here. For a month.
And anything's possible. . .'

Anything's possible. . . The words whispered around
and around in her head, and she knew that Lloyd
Neale was mixed up in there somehow.

Lloyd Neale. . .

She shook herself angrily as she placed clothes on
hangers in her new wardrobe. Leave him out of it, she
told herself. He's a grumpy, arrogant male, engaged
to another woman. Why on earth do you keep thinking
about him?

She had no answer.

The kitchen staff gave her dinner, and subjected her
to a thorough inquisition as she ate. Sally enjoyed it,
but knew that the sooner she had her own kitchen
organised, the better. She wasn't too keen on eating
with five pairs of eyes watching every spoonful.

Seven o'clock. Sally pulled her concert tickets from
her pocket and looked at them thoughtfully before
going along to Midwifery to knock on Gina's door.

Gina was perched happily in bed with her new
daughter in her arms, Lisa beside her, and her husband
hovering paternally over them all. Sally smiled at the
little family.

51

'What a picture of domestic bliss. How's wee Sarah, then?'

'You mean Pumpkin,' Gina laughed. 'She's been known as nothing else since she was born. Four hours old and already nicknamed. Oh, Sally. . .'

Sally walked forward to inspect the crumpled bundle. 'They don't look very much at this stage, do they?' She smiled and was met with a chorus of disapproval. Lisa though, choked on a giggle.

'She's so wrinkled.' The little girl grinned. 'She looks like a red prune. I wasn't game to say it until you did, Sally, but she does.'

'Goodness,' Gina laughed, 'Pumpkin, I don't mind. But prune. . . And Lisa, I don't think you should be addressing our new surgeon as "Sally".'

Sally smiled and her fingers touched Lisa lightly on the hair as she shook her head. 'I'd prefer her to call me Sally,' she told Lisa's parents. 'It makes me feel less of an ancient surgeon and more like I've made at least one friend in this place. And I came to ask if my new friend was busy tonight.'

Gina and Struan looked at each other and Lisa's face set.

'Miss Howard's been here,' the child said tightly. 'She said Gina and Dad would be better off without me and she wanted to take me to her place. But Dad said I should stay.'

'Of course.' Sally flipped the ponytail affectionately as she watched the pain on Lisa's face. Dratted woman. She'd expected no subtle approach from Margaret Howard. The woman Lloyd Neale had asked to marry him was as subtle as a sledge-hammer—and just about as warm. 'But I've a feeling your Gina should be asleep,' Sally added softly. 'She's been working so hard, Lisa.'

'I am tired,' Gina confessed. 'And Struan hasn't even done a ward-round yet. He has about three really ill patients to see before he gets to bed tonight.'

'I'll stay in the waiting-room while he works,' Lisa said stubbornly. 'Or I'll sit here and not say a word and Dad can take me home when he's finished.'

'You can do that.' Struan placed his hand reassuringly on his daughter's shoulder. 'Margaret's wrong when she said we don't want you. You know that, Lisa, love. But if Sally's offering something really good. . .'

'I'm not sure if I am.' Sally produced the tickets and handed them to Lisa. 'The thing is, I have two tickets to this concert and no one to go with. I thought. . . Maybe, if you're not too busy. . .'

'You're not just saying this to keep me out of the way?' Lisa demanded, taking the tickets suspiciously, and Sally smiled.

'Out of the way of Gina snoring? I might be doing you a favour.' She chuckled at Gina's expression. 'It doesn't matter, Lisa. If you don't want to come with me, there's an end to it. It's probably too late a night for you if you've school tomorrow—only it does seem a shame to tear the ticket up.'

Lisa stared down at the ticket, suspicion slowly fading. 'This group's supposed to be really good,' she said slowly. 'They were advertised in the paper, but Dad said we couldn't go because we didn't know what Gina would be doing.' She looked up at Sally. 'Did you know I learn violin?'

'I didn't know that. Does that mean you'd like to come?'

Lisa stared at Sally for a long moment, as though testing her sincerity. What she read in Sally's face seemed to reassure her and she turned to Struan.

'Can I go?' she asked her father, and Struan nodded.

'Of course you can, Lisa, love. You'll be far happier with Sally than sitting in the waiting-room waiting for me. Grandma will arrive tomorrow and you and she

can look after each other until Gina comes home. But
for tonight. . .' His eyes met Sally's in an expression
of gratitude. 'For tonight, being with Sally might be
more fun than being here. And you should have a
night out to celebrate Pumpkin's arrival.'

The child nodded, satisfied. She slid off the bed and
put a hand in Sally's. 'OK,' she announced. 'I'd love
to come, Sally. When do we go?'

'Right now.'

'I look like being in the hospital for another three
or four hours,' Struan told Sally. 'If you could bring
her back here. . .'

'Lisa will have to bring me,' Sally told him. 'Or at
least direct me. As yet I haven't a clue where I am in
this town. OK, Lisa, my love. Let's go. You're about
to introduce me to my very first taste of Gundowring's
social life.'

It was a very satisfactory night. Both Lisa and Sally
enjoyed the concert—the quartet more than living up
to their excellent reputation—and then Lisa took Sally
to the town's pancake parlour for supper. They ate
huge raspberry sundaes and stacked pancakes with
maple syrup, and then drove back to the hospital in
sated bliss.

'Wow,' Lisa said sleepily. 'A baby and pancakes too.
That was great, Sally.'

'I agree,' Sally told her. 'I think we should do it
again some time soon.'

'How about tomorrow?' Lisa asked, and giggled as
Sally rolled her eyes.

'If I do that more than once a month they'll have
to widen the doors to let me through.' Sally stopped
the car and ushered the little girl into the darkened
hospital.

Where would Lisa's father be?

Sally turned towards Reception to ask, and then

turned again at the sound of familiar halting footsteps. Lloyd. . .

He limped through into the reception area and stopped dead when he saw her. 'What the. . .? What on earth are you doing with Lisa?' His voice was incredulous.

'Sally took me to a concert,' Lisa said happily, her voice blurred with the beginnings of sleep. She made an ineffective dab at a spot of raspberry ice-cream on her nose and looked up at Sally with affection. 'And it was delicious. . .'

'You took Lisa to the concert. . .' Lloyd hadn't moved. He stood ten feet from them, his face expressionless as he stared at Sally. 'The concert we had tickets for? Margaret said Lisa was staying with Gina.'

'Lisa preferred the concert.' Sally kept her voice calm, but it was a struggle.

'But——'

'But Lisa didn't wriggle—or, at least, she didn't wriggle any more than I did—and she didn't unwrap one sticky lolly.' Sally allowed a trace of a smile to creep back into her eyes. 'So I'm not about to be run out of town, Dr Neale.'

Lisa looked up at Sally, confused by her words. 'But. . . Weren't you. . .? Weren't you supposed to take me, Sally?'

'Of course I was supposed to take you,' Sally said roundly, her eyes still locked on to Lloyd's. 'But some people have funny ideas about kids. Sometimes they almost forget they're people. Have you ever noticed that?'

'Like talking about me as if I'm not there?' Lisa nodded thoughtfully. 'Yeah. . .'

'I don't. . .' Lloyd's eyes blackened with anger. 'I don't do that to you, Lisa.'

'Of course you don't,' Lisa said scornfully. 'But some

people do. Miss Howard does. All the time.' Then she looked behind Lloyd as someone else approached. 'Daddy!'

Struan swept his tired daughter up in his arms. 'Hi, poppet. Brilliant timing. Lloyd and I have just finished coping with a nasty asthma attack. Had a good time?'

'Excellent,' Lisa said sleepily. 'Can we go home now?'

'When you've thanked Sally.'

'I already have,' Lisa said sleepily. 'Three times. Or maybe four. I can't remember. . .'

A minute later they were gone. Lloyd and Sally were left in the deserted waiting-room, their eyes still locked.

'How's Mr Butler?' Sally asked slowly. The air around them was thick with undercurrents she didn't quite understand. There was anger, but there was something else as well.

'I checked him fifteen minutes ago. I've sedated him as much as I dare, and he seems to be settled. I daren't take the intubation tube out, though. There's still tar sticking to the roof of his mouth. The air ambulance will pick him up at nine tomorrow morning.'

'Will you go with him?' For an intubated patient it was essential that a doctor be available at all times.

'They have a doctor on board.' Lloyd grimaced. 'I'd like to go—if he's on a respirator then he really should have an anaesthetist on board—but then there's no anaesthetist here until I get back.'

'And that's a risk.'

'Yes.' Lloyd dug his free hand into the pocket of his white coat, weariness showing in the gesture. 'And with Gina out of action and Struan preoccupied. . .' He sighed. 'Well, at least we seem to have ourselves a surgeon who doesn't fall to pieces in emergencies.'

'Well, well,' Sally said lightly, trying to disguise her pleasure at the words. 'Does that mean I've moved up a notch? Next step up from gift-horse?'

He stared at her for a long moment and then his tired eyes relaxed a little.

'I didn't call you that.'

'No.' Sally smiled and then foraged into her hand-bag. 'But I guess I still am—and I pay my bills. Sixty dollars, Dr Neale.'

The softening faded from his eyes. 'Keep it.'

'But you're saving for your house of dreams,' Sally teased gently. 'I'd hate to see you go a brick short because I forgot to pay my bills.'

His teeth almost audibly ground. 'For heaven's sake. . .'

She smiled apologetically. 'I'm joking. But, please, I'd hate Margaret to think I hadn't paid.' She handed over the money and then stood for a moment, looking up at him. There was a human being behind that aloof mask—if only she could reach him. 'Are you. . .are you going to bed now?'

Her abrupt question startled Lloyd. The anger faded a little. 'No. I have. . . There's a child in the kids' ward with severe asthma. I'll stay awake for another hour until I'm sure she's over the worst.'

'Well, then. . .' Sally fought for courage and found it. Talk about taking the bull by the horns. . . 'Look, I'm tired, Lloyd, at least tired of standing in one spot, and I'm aching for coffee.' The thought was impulsive, probably stupid, but impossible to retract now. 'Would you like to have coffee with me? I had pancakes with Lisa, but I'm desperate for caffeine and I've unpacked my percolator.'

There was a long moment's silence. Sally watched with interest, trying not to care if he said no.

'Why?' he said at last.

Good grief! Why?

Frantically Sally searched for something to say. Anything. Finally her sense of humour came to the rescue.

'Because. . .because I'm planning to ravish you.'
She managed a wry, self-mocking smile. 'I'd say come
and see my etchings, but you know I haven't had time
to hang them.'

'Dr Atchinson. . .'

His reaction made her laughter surface. Sally's smile
lit her eyes, laughter twinkling within. 'Actually, I
make a point of never ravishing engaged men,' she
assured him. 'Honest! But I am heading for coffee,
and you look like a man who could use some. So—
would you like some coffee?'

He stared at her for a long moment. 'Margaret will
be hurt when she finds you took Lisa to the concert,'
he said at last.

Sally's laughter faded. She nodded slowly. 'I guess
she might be, and I'm sorry that she'll be hurt,' she
told him, 'but I can't help it.'

'I beg your pardon?' His eyebrows were at his hair-
line. Clearly this man wasn't used to being addressed
like this by those junior to him.

'Margaret did her fair share of hurting,' Sally said
solidly. 'She as much as told Lisa she wouldn't be
wanted now her adoptive parents had their own baby.
If she can inflict pain like that without thinking, then
I can't be too careful of her feelings when I'm trying
to undo the damage.'

'She didn't mean to be hurtful.'

'I know. She only acted for the best. But
sometimes. . . Sometimes that's worse than doing
nothing at all.'

His lips tightened. 'I don't need you to be giving me
a lesson on morality,' he snapped.

'I'm not giving you one.' Sally shrugged her
shoulders. 'I'm not even intending to give your
fiancée one—much as she deserves it.'

'That's enough.'

Sally raised her eyebrows in polite uninterest. 'Is it,

Dr Neale? Are you going to send me to my room without dinner for impolite behaviour? It's too late. I'm full of pancakes.'

'Sally Atchinson. . .' His fury exploded and his hands came out and gripped her shoulders. Unheeded and unneeded, his stick clattered to the floor.

'Yes?' Wide, innocent eyes gazed up at him, and only Sally knew what an effort it cost her to suppress a shudder at his touch. And it wasn't revulsion that was making her shudder.

They stood, absolutely still. His hands tightened on her shoulders until they hurt, but Sally didn't let her gaze waver.

'You know,' she said conversationally, and heaven knew the effort it cost her to keep her voice calm, 'you know, you seem to drop that walking-stick any time you want to, and you don't appear to be leaning on me at the moment. Do you really need it? How long since you had physiotherapy?'

'I beg your pardon?'

'How long——?'

'That's none of your business.'

'No,' Sally said sadly. 'I bet it isn't anybody else's business, either. If you had a regular doctor, I think he'd be telling you your foot drags because you haven't finished a course of rehabilitation. Am I right?'

'I said——'

'I heard you. It's none of my business. But if you won't have rehab and you're letting your foot drag, and helping it by using a stick, then you'll just compound the problem. Even my surgical training's told me that. If you don't intend keeping up with physiotherapy, then I'd try not to use the stick. It has to force strength into your leg if you don't have the stick's extra support.'

His breath hissed in and his hands tightened. His fingers hurt.

'I don't need your diagnosis, Dr Atchinson.'

'I'm just trying to be helpful.' Sally looked up into angry eyes that were too close for comfort, and her heart lurched within. 'It's my job.'

'To care for patients who need help.'

'And you don't?' Sally wrinkled her nose. 'How can you say you don't need help when you're engaged to Margaret?'

She'd done it now. The fuse was lit and hissed towards the target, racing to explosion. Lloyd's face was dark with anger. He looked almost as if he wanted to hit her, Sally thought, but he couldn't do that if he kept hold of her shoulders.

She didn't turn away. Her eyes stayed on his, meeting his with a challenge that couldn't be ignored.

The hold tightened. The anger intensified until Sally felt it as a physical thing. It was more than anger, though, Frustration. . . Fury. . . Knowledge that she spoke the truth. And something more.

The fingers on her shoulders pulled her forward. Sally didn't flinch. She held her face up as she realised what was starting to be inevitable. A kiss of anger. . .

No. Not with Lloyd Neale's rigid code of conduct. He didn't run in hospital precincts. He wouldn't kiss in anger—or kiss in any mood at all. Not when he was engaged to another woman.

Sally was thrust back with a savage oath—so sharply that she almost fell. She staggered back and her hand went instinctively to her lips as she found her footing— as if she'd already felt Lloyd's mouth on hers.

There was a long, long silence. Finally Lloyd swore beneath his breath and bent to retrieve his stick. He stood straight again and stared down at her, as if she were some sort of malevolent wasp.

'I don't want your coffee,' he said softly, his voice dripping ice. 'I don't believe I want anything from you, Dr Atchinson, except your departure as soon as I can arrange it. This month's going to seem like a lifetime.'

'I hope so, Dr Neale,' Sally said softly—too softly to be heard—her fingers still on her lips as he turned and limped away. 'If a month's all I've got, then I hope it seems like a lifetime.'

Sally slept badly. Her bedroom was strange—the murmur of the surf below the hospital in ears used to the hum of city traffic was unfamiliar enough to pierce her dreams—and Sally certainly dreamed.

She didn't dream of surf, though. Sally's dreams were full of Lloyd Neale. His angry face stayed with her as she tossed and turned, and in the morning she felt she'd hardly slept at all.

Drat the man! Why did his face have to pierce her thoughts with such intensity? She was behaving like a moonstruck teenager—and here she was almost thirty. Sally surveyed herself in the bathroom mirror as she dried her bright curls, and wrinkled her nose at her reflection.

'Leave the man alone,' she told her reflection. 'He doesn't want anything to do with you. He certainly doesn't want professional advice—what on earth were you thinking of to offer it? He's happy with his limp and his dowdy, sour-faced fiancée—so for heaven's sake, Sally Atchinson, stop thinking about him!'

It wasn't as easy as it sounded. Sally adjusted her white coat—new for her first morning's official duties—and set forth, only to find Lloyd in the first ward she visited.

Henry, their tar-coated patient from the night before, was still in Intensive Care. A nurse sat beside him, watching the monitors, but by the movement of his hands as Lloyd talked to him Sally could see he was at least semi-conscious.

Lloyd was frowning over Henry's obs chart and Sally peeped over his shoulder to see as well. He flashed her a glance of annoyance and thrust the chart at her.

'Look all you like, Dr Atchinson.'

'Thank you,' Sally said cheerfully, determined not to let his sour mood dull her day. She read the chart with care, cheered by the absence of anything of interest, and then moved up the bed to take Henry's hand. Behind her, Lloyd said nothing.

'Hi, Henry,' Sally said softly. Henry was so heavily sedated that it was doubtful he'd hear her, but if he could then nothing would be so frightening as to have people moving around and not know who or where they were. Especially when his eyes were so completely closed. 'You don't know me, but I'm Sally Atchinson, the town's new surgeon.'

'I've told Henry about you,' Lloyd said heavily, and Sally flashed him an insincere look of gratitude. I'll bet, she thought.

'I'd like to check your mouth,' Sally went on, ignoring the interjection. 'It'd be much more comfortable for you to get this tube out—and maybe if there are no burns to your throat then we could.' She flashed a look at Lloyd. 'What do you think, Dr Neale?'

'There's still bitumen inside the mouth,' Lloyd told her, his professional self fronting for the first time. He moved to the other side of the bed. 'I think you must have gulped a bit into your mouth as it hit, Henry. Either that or opened you mouth as it splashed down. There seems to be a bit of tar on the roof of the mouth, but I can't see any lower down. If the choking was because of warm bitumen coming loose from the face then there's no problem—and the ease with which we slid in the breathing tube suggests there's little oedema.'

There was no response from Henry. It must be dreadful, Sally thought, to be deprived of sight and speech in one fell swoop. If they could get the tube out. . .

'I'm just going to feel,' she told Henry, touching his arm in a gesture of reassurance. She smiled up at Lloyd. 'I'd let Dr Neale do it, but his fingers are three times as big as mine.'

Lloyd nodded wordlessly, and watched as Sally's fingers gently explored the injured mouth. She lit the roof of the mouth and bent to see, her eyes carefully assessing.

'There's only one piece of tar still here,' Sally said at last. 'It's adhered to the roof of the mouth. I think. . .I think we might risk trying to loosen it. There seems to be nothing down further.' She looked down at the obs. Henry had been given morphine half an hour ago. It was the perfect time to do it. 'What do you think?'

'I'd be happier for Henry to be breathing by himself on the trip to Melbourne,' Lloyd agreed. Last night's anger was put aside with professional detachment. He glanced at his watch. 'We have two hours before the plane arrives. If we get rid of the tube now we have a chance to see how he goes before we hand him over.'

'OK.' It was a risk, Sally acknowledged. If there was swelling of the throat then they'd have to reinsert the tube—but the swelling would be obvious as they tried to take it out.

'Right.' Lloyd was obviously ahead of her in planning. 'We get rid of the tar in his mouth first, though. It's no use getting rid of the tube and having some of that muck work its way loose and choke him again.'

'I hoped you'd agree, Dr Neale. Sister's just finding us some peanut oil and kerosene now.'

What followed was tedious, painstaking work, applying the tar over and over again with the mix of the oil and kerosene, waiting until it loosened, applying more. . . If they hurried—if they tried to pull, rather than wait until the bitumen softened—then they could deepen the burn. Henry's whole face had to be done

eventually, Sally knew, and her heart wrenched in
sympathy with the burned man.

As each millimetre of bitumen came off, Sally
checked the burn, fearing it would get deeper. It didn't
happen, though. The tar must have been cooled by
the moisture in the man's mouth—or maybe it had
been sucked in after the initial thrust of hot tar. The
burns were only partial thickness, and the bitumen
came clear without further damage.

'Do you think we should go further?' she asked
Lloyd. He was soaking swabs in the oil-kerosene mix-
ture and handing them to Sally one at a time. With
her small, skilled surgeon's hands, she was the perfect
person to perform this task, and Lloyd had conceded
that immediately. Now, as Sally lifted the last tiny
piece of bitumen clear of Henry's mouth, she looked
down into the bowl of black matter with satisfaction.
'Maybe we could clear the eyes. . .'

'No.' Lloyd shook his head. 'That's a job for
Melbourne. We've stressed Henry enough for now.'

Sally nodded. Surgery was her forte, but it was up
to Lloyd, the physician, to assess the likely strain
on Henry.

'Let's get his mouth completely clean now,' Lloyd
said. The last thing they wanted was for kerosene to
end up in Henry's lungs. There might well be tar there
already—but that was for the doctors in Melbourne
to assess.

They went to work again, carefully ridding the
mouth of any trace of oil and kerosene while the
breathing tube was still in place.

'Right,' Sally said finally, satisfied at last that
the mouth was clean. 'I think we're ready to go.'

'OK.' Carefully, Lloyd reversed the relaxant. As its
effects wore off, Sally saw the man's chest heave as
he fought to breathe for himself. His hands started to
move to rid himself of the tube. Sally's hands caught

his and she held him firmly while Lloyd deflated the cuff and carefully pulled out the tube.

For a couple of moments there was silence, except for harsh rasping as Henry made his throat work again.

'I think we might try a sip of water.' Lloyd lifted a beaker and, with a nod to Sally, the two lifted Henry into a half sitting position and Lloyd placed the glass against the tar-coated lips.

Henry was more than ready. He sucked the fluid down with the eagerness of a newborn calf after his first taste of milk, and the rasping breath was replaced with a sigh.

'Geez. . .' It was a croak of pleasure, laced with pain. To make his voice work was obviously a huge effort. 'Geez. . .'

'Don't try to talk, Henry,' Lloyd told him. 'Your throat will be sore after the tube—and there are burns in your mouth.'

He glanced up at Sally. 'Thanks for your help, Dr Atchinson. I'll write up instructions for Henry's transport. I'm sure there are other things you need to be doing.'

It was a clear dismissal. Sally flushed scarlet. Then she bit her lip. Drat the man. . . She was darned if she'd let him rattle her.

'There sure are,' she said cordially. 'All Gundowring's ingrown toenails, just waiting for Gundowring's new surgeon.' She gripped Henry's hand in hers. 'The best of luck in Melbourne, Henry. I'll be telephoning to find out how you're getting on, and looking forward to having you back here.' She flashed a bright smile at Lloyd's grim face and swept from the ward.

It was only when the door closed behind her that she found she was trembling.

So now what?

A surgeon with nothing to do. She had a couple of

people booked to see her during the morning—
referred by the local doctors yesterday afternoon—
and Mr Hammer's hernia, but she was hardly fully
occupied. She would be busy soon enough, she
guessed, but for now. . .

For now she'd go and see Gina—the only other
patient in this hospital she had any excuse at all to visit.

She found Gina finishing a feed. The new mother
laid her sleepy bundle back in the cot beside the bed
and smiled happily up at Sally.

'How's our new surgeon?' she asked, and Sally
grimaced.

'Dare I say a bit bored?'

'Well, that won't last.' Gina surveyed Sally's face
thoughtfully. 'Didn't you sleep well?'

'Hey,' Sally laughed, perching on the end of the bed.
'I'm the doctor. You're the patient.'

'Yeah, sure.' Gina's eyes didn't leave Sally's face.
'Struan tells me you and Lloyd haven't exactly hit
it off.'

'You could say that,' Sally agreed ruefully. 'He
thinks I'm flighty.'

'And you're not?'

'Well. . .' Sally grinned down at the woman she was
fast thinking of as a friend. 'I might be a little bit. But
I never go very high.'

'Just too high for our Dr Neale. . .'

'You're right there.' Sally shook her head. 'Goodness, Gina, what's eating the man?'

'You mean, why is he grumpy?'

'Yes. And why does he act older than any doctor
in this hospital—when he's not much more than thirty?
And as for that woman he intends to marry. . .'

'She's awful,' Gina agreed. 'A woman of duty, virtue
and not one scrap of human compassion.'

'Or humour.'

'Or humour,' Gina agreed. She looked up at Sally,

her eyes searching her new friend's face. 'So why does Lloyd worry you?'

Sally shrugged. 'I don't. . .'

'You're attracted to him?'

'No!'

'No?'

Sally opened her mouth to deny once again, but her denial died on her lips. Gina saw too darned much. She spread her hands. 'It just. . . It just seems there's someone special in there—if only he'd show it.'

'There sure is.' Gina lay back on her pillows, her hands behind her head and her expression softened. 'Lloyd Neale is a wonderful man, Sally Atchinson.'

'So your daughter tells me. Why?'

Gina was silent. The sound of the sea drifted in from the open window and it seemed as if it were taking her back—through memories that were painful as well as treasured.

'Lloyd was a young doctor when I arrived here first,' Gina said at last. 'Young. . . Young in heart and mind. I remember being astounded to find he'd already done his first part anaesthetics and wasn't much younger than me—he seemed such a kid. He loved life. He loved his medicine, and his patients thought the world of him. There was nothing he wouldn't do for them, too. An idealistic young man. Then. . .'

'Then?'

'Then I arrived. The night I hit town I pulled off the road to admire the view and was attacked by a mob of thugs. Lloyd came to my resuce and had his spine fractured for his efforts.'

'You're kidding. . .'

'Never more serious,' Gina said softly. 'You don't know how hard it is to think someone may never walk again because of you. Still, he did recover.'

'Not completely.'

'No.' Gina shook her head. 'The spark was extin-

quished for a while. He suffered a lot. And then. . .
Then, when we were starting to think we had our
Lloyd back, Lloyd's younger brother persuaded his
parents to mortgage their home to help in a business
venture. The business crashed. Lloyd's brother com-
mitted suicide and Lloyd was left trying to bail his
parents out of a financial and emotional nightmare.
It knocked the final spark of fun out of him. And
then. . .'

'Don't tell me,' Sally whispered. 'He met Margaret.'

'How did you guess?' Gina grimaced. 'Margaret is
safe, worthy, conscientious. . . She's filling a need for
Lloyd that he hardly acknowledges he has.'

'So she's making him happy?'

'No.' Gina's eyes suddenly flashed anger. 'She's
cementing his view that happiness is for the
frivolous few.'

Silence. Sally started out of the window at the
glistening sea.

'Why does he use a stick?' she asked at last. She
turned back to the bed to find Gina staring at her in
astonishment.

'You're quick,' the woman in the bed said. 'You
mean you noticed that he hardly needs it?'

'I noticed.' There was no need to tell Gina exactly
how she had noticed. The stare would become a goggle
if she did.

Gina shrugged. 'Well, you're right. He was going to
Melbourne once a month for intensive rehabilitation,
but after his brother suicided he stopped going. His
foot's still dragging. It'll take time to get it past that
point, but I don't think he ever will. It's as if. . . Well,
to be without a limp he might start enjoying himself
again. Fate worse than death. . .'

'It doesn't make sense,' Sally said slowly.

'It doesn't, does it?' Gina agreed. She smiled up at
Sally and her eyes held a hint of mischief. 'It really

needs someone to sort out the mess. How fortunate it is that Struan, Lesley and I seem to have hired just the woman for the job.'

where she belonged. Even when she spent the entire

CHAPTER FIVE

JUST the woman for the job. . .

The phrase echoed through Sally's head time and
time again over the next three weeks as she found her
feet in the busy practice. Sally's lack of occupation had
lasted a whole two hours on that first morning. Then
her first Theatre case had been due and Sally's leisure
time was at an end. She was busier than she had ever
been in her life.

And she was happier. At last Sally was doing initial
assessments of her own. She spent her time buzzing
from consulting-room to Theatre to wards, and the
mechanics of city practice, which had almost made her
give up her beloved surgery disappeared into the
realms of a bad dream. Over.

This was the surgery she had trained for. No longer
was the person on the operating table just number six
on her list for the morning. Number six was Muriel
Jeffries, with a nasty case of gallstones, two spoiled
cats and a penchant for bringing her grateful surgeon
freshly baked sponge cakes at every visit.

Despite a surfeit of sponge cakes, Sally listened to
patient histories with real enjoyment. Her only cloud
was the knowledge that she was being watched.

As the new doctor in town, Sally was aware that all
eyes were on her, but one pair of eyes was different.

Lloyd Neale watched her with cool contempt for
those three weeks, as though waiting for the bubble
to burst. His attitude was still that she was frivolous
and irresponsible—out for an easy life. It was only a
matter of time, his eyes said, before she tired of rural
practice and took her fun-loving self back to the city

where she belonged. Even when she spent the entire night operating and managed to smile at her patients in the morning, Lloyd's expression told her that he knew it was an act. Sooner or later, she'd be exposed for what she was.

It hurt. Sally tried hard to ignore his attitude, but sometimes it really was hard to keep her bright smile in place. Sometimes, when she had finished operating and turned to thank her anaesthetist, sometimes the coldness in his eyes made her feel chilled to the bone.

It shouldn't affect her. There were other doctors Sally hadn't agreed with in the past—and none of them had made her feel like this.

So snap out of it, Sally Atchinson, she told herself grimly as she started her evening rounds three weeks after her arrival. It's time he stopped bothering you.

She swung open the door of Men's Rehab and stopped dead. Lloyd was already here.

They'd made a tactical, unspoken agreement to do their ward-rounds as separately as possible—or rather, it seemed that Lloyd knew when Sally was likely to be in the wards and carefully avoided her. Every other doctor in the place greeted Sally with pleasure. If Lloyd could help it, he didn't greet her at all. It was almost unheard of now for Sally to bump into Lloyd in the wards.

Lloyd was standing at the bed of a patient Sally didn't recognise—a big, middle-aged man with recent burn scars spread over his face. To Sally's astonishment, Lloyd turned to her and smiled directly into her eyes as the ward door swung closed behind her.

'Dr Atchinson.' It was almost as if he'd been waiting for her to arrive.

'Y-yes?' Sally walked forward slowly, the surprise showing in her face, but Lloyd had turned to look back down at the man in the bed.

'I guess you don't remember this lady, Henry. She's

the one who suggested we leave your bitumen intact.'

Henry. . . Henry Butler. . .

Sally gasped in delight. The big man was looking up at her with bright, unclouded eyes. She'd heard from Melbourne that his sight hadn't been impaired, but until this moment she'd hardly believed it. He'd been in such a mess.

'Hey, welcome back.' She smiled down at him. She bent to look closely at his face. 'I can't believe it. Not even a skin graft?'

'One at the back of my neck,' Henry said bitterly. 'You know why? Because I scratched a bit of the bloody bitumen loose on the way down to Melbourne and took the last layer of skin off. If I hadn't done that, then I'd be home now. Thanks to you two.'

'Well, we didn't do much.' Sally flicked Lloyd a mischievous smile. 'As little as possible, is our motto. Isn't that right, Dr Neale?'

To her astonishment, Lloyd chuckled. His delight was as great as Sally's was, she realised.

'I'm only sorry this is going to stop me going to your "Welcome to Gundowring" dance,' Henry was saying. 'I wouldn't have missed it for quids otherwise. The missus tells me it's going to be a real shindig.'

Sally's face clouded momentarily and she flicked a glance upward at Lloyd. The dance had been a source of conflict. Gina and Struan had organised it, but Sally had heard from about five sources that Lloyd had been bluntly opposed to the idea.

'She's here for a month's trial,' he had expostulated. 'It's only three weeks. How do we know if she's here to stay?'

Lloyd had been howled down, Sally's delighted informants had told her.

'Doc Maitland said you were the best thing to happen to Gundowring since his wife arrived,' Matron had told Sally roundly. 'He says you're here to stay—and that's what we all hope, too, dear.'

So did Sally. Now, though. . . She looked up at Lloyd's fading smile, and once more the lonely cloud that had been drifting around her ever since she had met this man washed over her.

'It doesn't matter, Henry,' she said gently. 'I'll have enough people to welcome me.'

'Yeah, well, I'm a pretty dab hand at the foxtrot.' Henry grinned. 'It'd give me real pleasure to spin you round the floor, girl, and that's the truth.'

'I'll hold you to that at the next hospital dance, then.' Sally was gently fingering the scars. 'Henry, these are terrific. You'll hardly scar.'

'I know that.'

'If the doctor on the plane had paid attention to his patient and stopped you worrying the edge of the bitumen, you'd have even less,' Lloyd said grimly. 'I should have gone with you myself on the flight down to Melbourne.'

There was anger in his voice and Sally shook her head.

'You can't be everywhere, Lloyd,' she said gently. 'And if you'd gone to Melbourne we would have been without an anaesthetist.'

'Thanks, but I don't need your reassurance.'

Sally's eyes flashed. 'Then you don't have it,' she snapped in anger. She bit her lip and then forced herself to smile down at Henry. 'Our Dr Neale does a fine job of taking the worries of the world on his shoulders. I guess it's his decision, so we can't make a difference by reassuring him.'

Henry looked from Sally to Lloyd's darkening face, and nodded slowly. 'Yeah, the whole town knows he takes life too seriously. You ought to do something about it, Doc Atchinson.'

Sally smiled, trying to ignore the anger palpating behind her. 'I do my best,' she managed to say lightly.

'Are you going to Doc Atchinson's dance?' Henry demanded of Lloyd, and Lloyd's face set. Clearly he was trying not to display anger in front of a patient—and he thought Sally's discussion of him in front of Henry was unprofessional. Which it was, Sally conceded, but then, maybe it was her only defence.

'Of course I'm going,' Lloyd said tightly. 'Margaret and I always perform our social obligations towards our colleagues.'

No matter how inferior. . . The words weren't spoken but they were clear none the less, and Sally flushed scarlet. What was it about this man that had him trying to hurt her at every possible opportunity? And why did it hurt so much?

Henry ignored the unspoken implication, though the big man's look of flickering doubt at Sally showed that he had recognised it.

'Well, I want you to dance with Doc Atchinson for me,' he told Lloyd stolidly.

'I don't dance.'

'Bull,' Henry retorted rudely. 'You don't dance fast, but I saw you not more than three months ago at the fund-raising dinner for the nursing home. You waltz a treat—nearly as well as me.' He grinned up at Sally. 'He does, too, Doc. You save a dance for our Doc Neale and tell me tomorrow if I'm wrong.'

'Dr Neale. . . Dr Neale has a fiancée to dance with,' Sally said uncertainly, and Henry snorted.

'Being his fiancée doesn't give Margaret Howard exclusive rights to the man. It won't hurt Doc Neale to grant you one dance—and my spies'll tell me tomorrow whether he did or not. If he don't. . .' The man looked from doctor to doctor, and his burn-marked face creased into a smile. 'If he don't, then I'll suffer a relapse. At three in the morning. You just see if I don't!'

*   *   *

A dance. . . .

Sally stood in front of her wardrobe that night and stared at its contents in indecision.

She hadn't been to a dance since her father died. Four months. . .

It still seemed wrong somehow. Even though the move to Gundowring had eased the ache to bearable proportions, Sally seemed a different woman now from the girl who had bought these dresses.

One by one, Sally held her evening dresses before her. She had lots of evening dresses. Until his death four months ago, Sally's father had often needed her to act as hostess while he entertained as Chairman of the National Theatre. When she hadn't been working, Sally had loved accompanying him. Between father and daughter there was a special bond which, so far, no other man had broken.

He had disapproved of the crimson silk—the dress she was holding up now.

'You don't look like my Sally in that,' he'd said when she'd worn it first. 'Fun, maybe, but hardly elegant.'

Maybe. Sally held it closer and her eyes flicked into a smile. This was the sort of dress Lloyd would expect her to wear, though. It was cut too low, and although its tightly fitting shape reached almost to her ankles, a side slit came up near to her thighs.

Goodness. She'd raise a few eyebrows in this. Was she brave enough?

'This town needs stirring,' she said out loud, but a tiny inner voice demurred. It's not Gundowring you're trying to stir. It's Lloyd Neale.

'Margaret will wear black—what's the bet?' she demanded of herself aloud, and wrinkled her nose at her reflection. So what?

'So. . .' Sally took a deep breath. She glanced at her conservative dresses, and then firmly shut the wardrobe door. 'He who dares. . .' she whispered. 'Wins?'

What on earth did she want to win?

She didn't know. Sally shook her head at her reflection as she slipped on the wicked dress. She was air-dreaming. She was air-dreaming nonsense.

Sally stirred Gundowring all right.

She knew as soon as she walked in the door that the dress was a mistake. Gundowring was country conservative, and this dress wasn't. It was sexy, provocative and fabulous. The first time Sally had tried it on she had gazed into the mirror and chuckled. It had felt deliciously daring.

Gundowring didn't chuckle, though. The town drew in its collective breath, and it took all Sally's courage not to bolt home and change. Gina was waving to her, though, from a table near the door. Sally met her eyes, took courage in both hands, and made her way over to her through the throng. The crowd parted like the Red Sea before Moses.

'Whew!' Gina was grinning from ear to ear. Her own dress was demurely matronly, in deference to the bassinet parked innocuously under her chair. 'Sally Atchinson, whose socks are you about to knock off?'

'Not mine, I hope.' Sally smiled. She glanced ruefully down at her plunging neckline. 'I can't afford to lose one scrap more cloth.'

'You can say that again.' Gina was shaking with laughter. 'Good grief, Sally, you'll take the town's bachelors by storm. I don't think this town's ever seen the likes of this.'

'And red hair, too.' Gina's husband was clearly enjoying Sally's entrance enormously. He poured Sally a glass of wine and pulled back a chair for her to sit down. 'Not that you'll have much time to sit wearing that,' he added with a grin.

'It'd be a shame if you did,' Gina decreed. 'Oh, good. Here's Lloyd and Margaret.' She chuckled.

'Boy, Margaret's eyebrows will hit the roof.'

They were destined for disappointment. Apart from one cool hello, Margaret was clearly ignoring Sally.

Margaret had taken Sally's decision to take Lisa to the concert as a personal insult, and had lost no opportunity to snub Sally at every opportunity since. Now she sat as far from Sally as possible on the big table of doctors and their partners, and motioned for Lloyd to do likewise. After one cool, appraising look, Lloyd did the same.

The anticipation died from the evening.

So what had I been hoping for? Sally asked herself miserably as she watched the engaged couple start a long and obviously serious conversation with Lesley Maine. Why am I feeling like this?

'Dr Atchinson?'

Sally turned to find a portly man in his forties bending over her chair with solicitous interest.

'Sally, this is Randolph Small.' Gina performed the introductions and Sally was bemused to find laughter in her friends voice. 'Randolph's our local dentist.'

'I'm delighted to meet you.' The big man was beaming from ear to ear with unabashed delight. 'Could I have the honour of this dance, Miss Atchinson?'

It was Sally's first invitation to dance, but certainly not her last. She was whisked from partner to partner, and whenever there was a momentary lull in the stream of young men waiting to meet her, Randolph Small was waiting with genial good humour. As the evening drew to a close it was becoming more and more obvious that Randolph was regarding her with a proprietary air.

'I do need to fulfil a few social obligations,' he informed her as a rock number drew to an end.

Sally had been aching to show what she could do—dancing fast to rock was a skill she had learned early and loved—but Randolph had clutched her to himself and foxtrotted with grim intent, oblivious both to the music and the state of Sally's toes.

Now he held her fast to his bulky figure in a gesture of pure right and looked around. 'Ah, there's Margaret,' he beamed. He smiled down at Sally. 'Margaret's my second cousin once removed on my father's side. I always dance with her at least once.' And before Sally could utter a protest he propelled her to the table where Lloyd and Margaret were sitting the dance out.

'Can I leave Sally with you, Lloyd, while I wheel my cousin round the floor?' Randolph demanded ponderously. 'I'm sure you'll be in good hands, Sally.' Then, before she could protest, he had taken Margaret and ushered her on to the dance floor. Margaret, Sally noted with grim humour, was wearing demure black.

'Whew. . .' Sally stared after the departing couple with misgivings. Randolph was showing every sign of being a potential suitor, and he was as likely to be deflected from his chosen intentions as a mountain.

'Congratulations, Dr Atchinson,' Lloyd said drily. 'You seem to have made a conquest.'

'Lucky me.' Sally glanced down at Lloyd and then quickly away again. The comparison between Lloyd and Randolph was almost ludicrous, and she felt a sudden, ridiculous compulsion to burst into tears. 'If you'll excuse me, I'll go and find a drink.'

'No.' Lloyd rose to his feet and his hand came out to take hers. 'We have an engagement, if I'm not mistaken, Dr Atchinson. Henry asked me to dance with you, Randolph's demanded it of me, and I'm a man who knows where his duty lies.'

'What a very gracious invitation.' Sally attempted to pull her hand away but found his grip only tightened. 'You're under no obligation to me, Dr Neale.'

'No. But this is a waltz—the only dance I can attempt with any success.'

'I don't see why the fact that they're not playing all

waltzes should stop you dancing,' Sally said bitterly. 'Randolph does two steps forward, two steps back for every dance. If he can do it. . .'

'Poor Sally.' Lloyd looked down at her, his eyes compassionate. 'I've been watching you. Sore toes?'

'I can't feel them any more.' Sally wrenched at her hand. 'Please. . .'

'I promise I won't stand on a single toe.' Lloyd's expression had changed. His smile had slipped, and his eyes were unfathomable. He looked down at her and his mouth twisted into a mocking smile. 'I don't move fast enough for one thing. Come on.'

She didn't have a choice. Leaving his stick by the table, Lloyd led her firmly out on to the dance-floor. Then he turned to her and took her decisively into his arms.

Dear heaven. . .

The sensation was indescribable. Sally felt her head whirl in a mist of weird emotions. She had never felt like this. Never! All this man had to do was touch her and he turned her into a gibbering schoolgirl.

The dance-floor was crowded, with every couple on the floor making the most of the last dance before the evening ended. There was no room to be anything but close.

Despite his injury, Lloyd was an excellent dancer. He held Sally close and moved slowly but skilfully through the throng of dancers. Sally was hardly aware of his lameness, and even that slight faltering in his step made him seem more. . .

More like him. More like the Lloyd Neale she had fallen head over heels in love with at first sight.

She almost gasped as the realisation of what she was thinking slammed home. Lloyd felt her stiffen and his hand came up to cup her chin, forcing her to look up at him.

'What is it, Dr Atchinson?'

'N-nothing. . .'

He was so near! So close! She could feel his heart beating under the smooth fabric of his dinner jacket. In the deep blackness of dinner suit and tie he was impossibly handsome, and the way his mouth twisted—the way his eyes looked down at her with an expression of quizzical humour. . . And the way his hands touched the bareness of skin where her dress fell away at the back. . .

Dear God. . .

He was still looking down at her. The sound of the music fell away and their movements became negligible in the crush of people. They might as well have been alone. Lloyd's hands held her close to him, and Sally thought she could melt into the warmth at her breast. She felt as one. One with this man—a man she hardly knew—a man who didn't like her and was engaged to another woman.

She looked wordlessly back up at him, and maybe something in her eyes betrayed what she was feeling. His deep eyes narrowed in concern, and Sally felt a shudder of pure terror run through her body. She had no way of coping with this. She didn't have a clue what was happening to her. She had never felt like this in her life—and she had nowhere to run.

'Dr Atchinson?'

A hand on her bare shoulder made Sally jump a foot within the confines of Lloyd's arms, and Lloyd's grip tightened. Like Sally, it seemed he had no wish for the rest of the world to intrude.

The hand was insistent, though, and so was the voice. 'Dr Atchinson. . .' A deep voice, with a hint of urgency, was pulling her away from her drifting sensations of wonder.

Reluctantly Sally twisted within the confines of Lloyd's arms to see who it was who was calling her. Sally turned her head to see that a man in a dinner jacket had pushed his way through the crowd and was waiting anxiously for her to respond. Lloyd let her twist but still held her, and the feel of his hold sent waves of hot sensation through her body.

'Y-yes?' She recognised the man as the appointed master of ceremonies for the evening.

'Dr Atchinson, I know this is your "Welcome to Gundowring" party, but it seems. . . It seems there's been a smash in the mountains behind the town. Two kids in a car. The ambulance is bringing them in now, but the driver's just radioed to say one of the kids looks dreadful. Sister said she was going to need you. She's just rung through now to say could we get you down to the hospital.'

'I'll come at once.' Sally was already pulling away from Lloyd, and his hands released her with something like lingering regret. She met Lloyd's eyes with difficulty, 'Thank. . .thanks for the dance, Lloyd, I'll tell Henry. . .I'll tell Henry you did what you were told. Could you make my excuses for me?'

'You might need help.' Gerard, one of the town's family doctors, was on duty in Casualty tonight, but Gerard wasn't competent to give an anaesthetic.

'I'll call if I do,' Sally promised. 'Enjoy. . .enjoy the rest of your night.'

'I'll give Randolph your regrets at being called away,' Lloyd promised with a wry smile. 'He'll be devasted, I'm sure.'

That smile stayed with Sally all the way from the dance-hall to the hospital. Impossible to forget it. Sally tried hard to think of the drama waiting for her with the ambulance, but all she could think of was Lloyd's eyes.

Then, as she stopped the car and walked towards the hospital entrance, the ambulance screamed along the road and into the hospital car park, and even Lloyd's smile was thrust from her mind.

This was a tragedy. A young couple lay on stretchers

in the back of the ambulance, and as each was lifted out on to waiting trolleys Sally's heart sank.

The girl should at least live. Her leg was a mangled mess—a compound fracture which looked as if it had been crushed between two enormous weights. She was whimpering in pain as the ambulance doors were opened, and then, as the stretcher was lifted down, her leg must have moved. She screamed once—a long, agonised scream. Sally caught the girl's shoulders and pressed back as she tried to sit up, but the movement was too much. The girl passed into blessed unconsciousness.

Two kids. . . Sally dragged her eyes from the unconscious girl and turned to the next stretcher. What she saw there made her feel sick to the stomach. The same massive weight had caught the boy across the abdomen. Sally lifted the sheet covering the boy and winced. She felt the faint, thready pulse and bit her lip, forcing her shocked mind to think.

'He's in shock,' she snapped. 'I want IV, plasma and cross-matching—fast! We'll take him straight through to Theatre.'

The nurses were already moving. One junior nurse gave a fleeting titter at the incongruity of Sally's evening dress as she came into Casualty, but a look at what they were facing drove the colour from the nurse's cheeks. Every thought of Sally's unsuitable dress was washed from her mind as she flew into action.

Gerard, the doctor on call, was inserting a drip in the girl's arm, but he looked uncertainly at Sally. 'What are we going to do, Sally? I can't help you with the boy.'

'No. If you can get the girl pain-free before she regains consciousness—check for other injuries first, though.' Sally thought fast as she inserted the IV line in the boy's arm. 'I might be able to help you with her sooner than I'd like. We might. . . We might not be able to do much here, anyway. Sister, can you contact Dr Neale?'

There was no need. Lloyd must have followed Sally as soon as she left the dance. She looked up and could have wept with relief at the sight of Lloyd stripping off his dinner jacket as he limped through the casualty door.

'What's the go, Sally?' Lloyd glanced from the injured boy to the unconscious girl and back again. He whistled soundlessly. 'Whew. . .'

'We operate,' Sally told him. 'Fast. The boy has massive internal bleeding. X-ray and then surgery.'

Lloyd was moving before Sally finished speaking. His orders rang out for anaesthetic requirements, and with relief Sally realised that she had someone more than competent to assist. They had performed routine surgery together in the past few weeks, but this was the first time she could see his skills for what they really were.

It didn't help.

The surgery took every ounce of Sally and Lloyd's skill. For three hours they fought desperately for the boy's life. The liver was so badly crushed that Sally despaired. She cut the damaged parts away, removed the ruptured spleen, lifted fragment of ribs from ruptured lungs and carefully, meticulously, repaired torn blood vessels. All the while Lloyd monitored the boy's air supply like a hawk, talking Sally through the moments when the monitors flickered and she faltered in uncertainty.

After three hours she was beginning to think that there might be a hope, and then, just as she took a deep breath to say 'close', the boy's heart stopped beating.

The resuscitation attempts were futile. Lloyd tried again and again, but finally Sally gestured him to stand back from the table. Bleakly she closed the gaping wound, knowing that the parents would want to bid their dead son farewell with dignity.

There was salt on her lips. Sally blinked the useless tears away. She didn't cry. She didn't.

When would she ever get used to this? And the last time this had happened. . . Memories of her last death on the operating table came flooding back, and it was all she could do to keep her knees steady under her.

This boy was eighteen, maybe—certainly little more. Sally looked up at his long lashes on his now closed eyes and felt like letting the tears flow freely.

She didn't. There was the family to face—and Lloyd, looking across at her with concern.

'Are you OK, Dr Atchinson?'

'Yes.' Sally shrugged hopelessly and turned away to the sink. 'Sister, we'd better clear this theatre. I'm going to have to do something about the girl's leg. How is she?'

'She's stable,' the senior nurse told her. 'We have her next door, waiting, but. . .'

'But?'

'The boy. . . The boy's parents are in the waiting-room.'

'And the girl's?'

'No. She's from Melbourne. We've contacted her parents, but they can't get here until morning. We told them to wait in Melbourne until they hear, as we might send the girl to the city.'

Sally nodded. She shrugged out of her theatre gown. 'I'll see the lad's parents, then.'

'Sally. . .'

Lloyd's voice cut through her misery and Sally hesitated.

'Yes?'

'Sally, I think I should talk to them.'

'Do you know them?'

'No.' Lloyd placed his hands on her sagging shoulders and forced her to look up at him. 'But you're in no condition to comfort parents.'

'I suppose. . .' Sally looked down at her blood-stained evening dress and winced. She looked like something out of a bad nightmare. 'I guess I look. . .'

'It has nothing to do with how you look,' Lloyd said gently. He beckoned to the senior nurse. 'Sister, get Dr Atchinson a strong, hot cup of tea with plenty of sugar. Sally, I'll see the boy's parents, and then we'll go and assess the girl together.'

'I'll go now,' Sally said wearily, but Lloyd shook his head. His hands came up to grip her shoulders hard.

'No. We see the girl together. You're not on your own here, Sally, no matter what your tired mind is telling you. Now, do as you're told.'

Sally looked up at Lloyd's concerned face and the despised tears threatened to return.

'Y-yes, Doctor,' she whispered, and he gave her a swift, reassuring smile.

'OK, Sally. This isn't the first tragedy you've faced and it won't be the last. You have the strength to face it, and to help others face it.'

'How do you know that?' Her voice was a thready whisper in the tragedy-laden silence.

'I'm learning,' he said softly. 'Given enough time, and I'm finally learning.'

CHAPTER SIX

SHE did have the strength to keep going. If it hadn't
been for the memory of that awful night four months
ago, Sally wouldn't have faltered, and Lloyd's strength
somehow hauled her through the pain.

The girl's leg had a compound fracture which was
cutting off all circulation to her foot. She'd need recon-
structive surgery in Melbourne if she wasn't to lose
her leg, but in the mean time it was Sally's job to
restore the blood supply to the lower limb.

They returned to the cleared theatre and started
again, pushing weariness aside as irrelevant.

It was dawn before Sally was satisfied that she'd
done all she could. Lloyd reversed the anaesthetic and
gave further morphine—'Let's keep her pain-free for
the flight'—and then signalled to the attendants that
she could be wheeled away.

By the time consciousness fully returned, the girl
would be in Melbourne, hopefully with parents
beside her.

'You don't think I should go with her?' Sally asked
wearily as she washed. 'Or you?'

'No. She'll be fine with the air ambulance doctor.
The leg's the only major injury and she's young and fit.'

'Still. . .' Sally looked reluctantly after the departing
trolley, and then sighed as she saw a uniformed figure
standing in the doorway. Police. Of course. After every
tragedy came the inquisition.

At least this wouldn't be like the last.

Sally pushed the unwanted thought aside and dried
her hands.

'Finished then, Doc?' The policeman was looking

anxiously from Lloyd to Sally and back again. 'I know you'll be tired, but I have to get details. . .'

'I understand.' Sally looked down at the ruins of her dress. 'I suppose it can't wait until I shower and change?'

'Come through to my apartment,' Lloyd said gently as the policeman shook his head. 'We'll be out of the sight of day staff coming on, and we can drink coffee while we answer questions.'

So Sally sat again at Lloyd's kitchen table, answering questions in an exhausted, dead voice while the policeman interrogated her as to the extent of the boy's injuries. The more questions he asked, the more the nightmare of four months ago returned. She cradled her mug of hot coffee and fought for a hold on reality, but more and more she felt it was slipping.

'Look, what is this?' Lloyd asked suddenly as the questions went on and on. Lloyd's eyes were resting on Sally, noting the weary slump of her shoulders and the strain on her voice. 'Surely we don't need this inquisition. Dr Atchinson's close to exhaustion—surely you can see that?'

'I know,' the policeman said apologetically. 'I wish this wasn't necessary. But I have to get a full report ready for homicide this morning.'

'Homicide. . .' Sally's eyes flew open. The nightmare slammed back in full. 'But. . . The boy was in a car accident. How can that be homicide?'

The policeman sighed and laid down his pen.

'Well, it depends what made the kids crash. It seems they're members of the anti-logging crusade camped up behind Mount Mendy. There's been a lot of bad blood between the kids and the loggers.'

'Because of the nails?' Lloyd demanded, and the policeman nodded.

'Nails?' Sally asked blankly.

'The kids are idealistic and on the losing end of the

conservation argument,' the policeman told her. 'A few weeks ago they decided to drive long nails into all the best timber. It makes the logs useless, as machinery disintegrates on contact with them. Unfortunately they failed to warn the loggers of what they'd done, and one of the men lost an eye when his chain-saw hit a nail and smashed.'

'Ugh.' Sally clutched her hot coffee tighter and stared into the depths of the brown liquid, visualising the injury the policeman was describing.

'The loggers were out for blood for a few weeks, but it seemed to settle down,' the policeman continued. 'Last night, though, young Melinda and Gary, the pair you've been working on, drove their car into the logging area after midnight. The kids at the camp say they heard the sound of gun-shots before they heard the car crash.'

'But. . .' Sally shook her head. 'Neither of them has gun-shot injuries.'

'The car has, though,' the policeman said grimly. 'I've been all over the car and one of the tyres has a neat bullet-hole in the tyre rim. It's my theory that a few more went home in the rubber, the tyre shredded and the car went over an embankment. It was going too fast—but then it would be if the kids were scared silly and someone was shooting at them.'

'So. . .' Lloyd nodded. 'A murder charge, then?'

'Manslaughter at least, if we can find who did it. I don't like our chances, though. The loggers will stick together like glue and there'll be alibis all round. I've already been told every logger in the place was drinking in their communal hall.'

'Poor, silly kids,' Sally said slowly. She felt sick. 'What a price to pay!'

Lloyd was watching her curiously. Now he stood and opened the door for the policeman.

'As you say,' he said flatly. 'Sergeant, if you've

finished, we've a long day ahead, and it's due to start about now. If you have any more questions, ring me later.' His emphasis was on the 'me', and his eyes held a direct message to the policeman. He nodded significantly at the exhausted Sally and his eyes told the policeman to leave. Now.

Even the policeman's duty was no match for those eyes.

He went.

'And now, Sally Atchinson.' Lloyd crossed to the table, lifted the mug from Sally's lifeless fingers and raised her firmly to stand before him. 'Would you like to tell me what's going on in your head?'

Sally looked blankly up at him. 'I don't. . .I don't know what you mean.'

'I think you do,' he said gently. 'You look as hunted as those kids. The more questions the policeman asked, the more you looked like a scared rabbit. Sally, what's made you look like that? What has frightened you so badly?'

Sally shook her head, tinglingly aware of the touch of his hands on her bare shoulders. There was an almost overwhelming compulsion to droop on to his chest and weep—to sink towards the comfort he seemed to be offering.

He was engaged to Margaret. There was no comfort for Sally with Lloyd Neale.

Somehow, he knew what she was thinking. 'I can still be a friend,' he said softly, and his voice was laced with a tightness Sally didn't understand. He cupped her face in his hand and drew her chin up until her exhausted eyes met his. 'Am I imagining it, or does the vivacious, impertinent Sally Atchinson have need of a friend?'

'No. Yes. . .' Sally pulled away from his hands and he released her. She backed a few feet from him and looked up, her heart twisted in confusion. 'I. . .I'm sorry,' she managed. 'It's just. . . Those poor kids. . .'

'They were damned fools for going back into the logging area,' Lloyd said bluntly. 'They knew the feelings of the loggers. The logger who lost his eye was well-liked, and he has a wife and four kids. If they were putting more nails in. . .'

'You don't know that.'

'No. But I know they shouldn't have gone in after midnight.'

'Maybe they believed in their cause absolutely,' Sally said sadly. 'It's a prerogative of the young.'

'And the foolish.'

Sally shrugged. 'Is it foolish?' she asked wearily. 'Isn't the saving of the rainforests worth risks?'

'That's idealistic fantasy.'

Sally looked up at him and her heart contracted in pure pain. 'And idealism isn't in your code of honour, Dr Neale?'

'I think I've grown out of it.'

'I hope I never do,' Sally said dully. She shook her head. 'Look, I'm not condoning kids putting nails in the trees. But, whatever they did, these kids don't deserve what came to them. Shooting their tyres out. . .' She broke off and turned away. 'If you'll excuse me, Dr Neale. . .I have surgery this morning. I have to do a long ward-round first and if I don't have a shower soon the blood on this dress will congeal into concrete. It's making me feel ill.'

'It's a darned shame,' Lloyd said softly. He crossed to where she stood with one limping stride and once more his hands touched her shoulders. 'It was a beautiful dress.'

'"Was" is the operative word.' Sally didn't pull from the feel of those hands. She didn't move. Just stood, defenceless and mute, waiting for pain. Why should the feel of those hands cause her such pain?

'Sally. . .'

'Yes?' It was hardly more than a whisper.

'Sally, what is it? What the hell's hurting you? What caused the pain while the policeman was questioning you? It wasn't just the loss of the boy. You looked. . . You looked frightened.'

'I'm not frightened.'

The heck she wasn't. Sally had never been more frightened in her life. Her heart was thumping at a rate that would make most doctors ring for the crash cart, and it was only because this man was looking at her—Lloyd was touching her, and his eyes were dark and warm and. . .

She was drowning. The fatigue, effort and despair of the last few hours slammed back in such a wave of emotion that she felt she would fall. She looked up into those eyes and she felt her knees give. Lloyd swore softly under his breath and his grip tightened.

'Hell, Sally, you're exhausted.' He swore again and then, with one fluid movement, he swept her up into his arms.

Sally caught at her confusion and exhaustion, and made one last despairing effort to collect her dignity.

'Put me. . . Put me down.'

'You'll fall over if I do.'

'I won't. . .' She struggled weakly against his encircling arms. 'You'll fall over. You can't support me on your leg.'

'You're the one who told me I should be using my leg more. Well, I'm about to. I'm about to carry you the full length of the hospital without the use of my stick. Will that satisfy you, Dr Atchinson?'

'You wouldn't. . . You wouldn't dare. . .'

'Watch me.'

He had no trouble at all. Lloyd pushed the door of his living-room open with his elbow and then carried the stunned Sally down the hospital corridors, past the bemused nursing staff as they performed their early

morning change-over, and straight into her apartment.
He hardly limped at all.

'Put. . . Put me down! Lloyd Neale, put me down
this minute!'

Sally hadn't spoken while she was in the hospital
corridor. There was only one thing worse than being
carried bodily through the hospital by Lloyd Neale,
and that was to be carried screaming. She'd never hear
the end of it.

She'd never hear the end of it now!

'I suppose you realise you've shot my reputation to
smithereens,' she faltered as he finally set her down
on unsteady feet. The door to her flat banged closed
behind them, cutting them off from interested spec-
tators.

'It'll survive,' Lloyd said curtly. 'I'm an engaged
man, remember.'

'I remember.'

The words were hardly a whisper. Sally stood, her
eyes level with his chin, and she couldn't look up for
the life of her. The tension between them was electric.

'Sally. . .'

'Y-you'd better go.'

'You need to be in the shower. Do you want help?'

'No!' It was a frightened whisper. 'Please, Lloyd. . .'

There was a long, long silence. It wasn't just tension
between them—it was something much more intan-
gible. It was as if there were a magnet, pulling each to
the other, pushing common sense aside and leaving. . .

And leaving only each other.

Sally finally looked up. The whirl of emotion within
settled into something more certain. There were problems which had to be faced—problems which made
this love difficult—but it was love that she was feeling.
This man was her mate. He was the man she belonged
with. The other half of her whole. . .

And Lloyd Neale—her love—was staring down at

her as if he was seeing a deep and frightening abyss. As if, by touching her, he would surely fall.

And yet he couldn't help himself. His hands came out to hold her slim waist, to draw her bloodstained body into him and to bend his face down so his lips met hers.

They were one. They were meant for each other. Their bodies melted together as if they were made to be joined. Sally's arms came up to tie behind his neck, pulling his mouth deeper to hers, and from a long, long way away she heard herself give a sob of pure joy.

Dear God, let this moment be forever. Let this feeling go on and on.

Sally had never felt anything like this. Her whole being was being swept away on a tide of emotion so strong she was threatening to drown. Her lips parted and his mouth possessed her. The taste of him. . . The feel. . .

This was her home.

Margaret.

Whether the thought crashed into her head or his first, afterwards she could never be sure. She only knew that suddenly the thought of Margaret was between them as surely as if Margaret herself was in the room, standing scornfully between them. They were suddenly feet apart, and Lloyd was looking at her as if he had been hit by a bullet.

'I can't. . .'

'I think. . .I think we just did,' Sally faltered. 'There's no can't about it. Oh, Lloyd. . .'

The shock on Lloyd's face faded and was replaced by a look of revulsion. 'Of all the stupid. . . Sally, I didn't mean——'

'You didn't mean to kiss me.' The strap on Sally's dress had slipped off her shoulder. She pulled it up and her fingers wandered higher, to touch her bruised lips. 'I guess. . .I guess not. After all, you're almost a happily married man.'

'I'm engaged to be married.'

Sally nodded. 'I had heard,' she said drily. She took a deep breath, searching for strength. Finally she turned and opened the door back out into the hospital.

'Then maybe you'd better leave, Dr Neale,' she said softly. 'Before. . .before we do something you might regret.'

The emphasis was on the word 'you'. Sally wouldn't regret anything. Not with this man. Not with her love.

The silence went on and on. Endless. The magnet was pulling with all its force, but Lloyd stood like stone. That was what his face looked like. Stone.

'Please. . .' Sally whispered finally. She felt drained of all emotion. She had nothing left to fight with. 'Please, Lloyd. I think. . . Please leave.'

He gave her one last hard, long look.

'I guess I was wrong,' he said heavily. 'No matter what you need, Sally Atchinson, I guess we can't be friends.'

By the time Sally emerged from her apartment, showered and suitably clad in demure dress and white coat, the hospital grapevine had done its work. Sally walked down the hospital corridor to be met by stunned silence, followed by giggles as soon as the nurses she passed turned out of sight.

Terrific. The grapevine was fairly humming. Dr Neale had been seen carrying Dr Atchinson down the hospital corridor at six-thirty in the morning—straight from his apartment all the way to hers—and she had still been in her bloodstained evening dress. Gundowring hospital was going to squeeze every last drop of enjoyment from the scenario that it could.

It had need of it, Sally acknowledged as she walked

from ward to ward to be met by bleak faces. The dead boy was the son of a local farmer. There were few patients in the hospital who didn't know him, and many were using the titillating piece of gossip about their new lady surgeon to drive away the bleakness of Gary's death.

'That dour-faced fiancée'd better have a look-out to her man.' Henry Butler grinned as she changed his dressing. 'And I heard he danced with you. She doesn't stand a chance with you around, Doc, and that's the truth.'

'He danced with me to obey your explicit instructions,' Sally said grimly. 'And he carried me through the hospital because I was tired.'

'Oh, yeah. . .' Henry hooted unbelievingly. 'Reckon I was born yesterday, Doc Atchinson? I can smell April and May when they're under my nose, and they're under my nose right now.'

By the time Sally fell into bed that night she was more exhausted than she had ever been in her life—and more confused. She fell asleep as her head hit the pillow, only to wake in the small hours of the morning to lie and stare at the ceiling, her head spinning with unanswerable questions.

Finally she rose and made her way through the stillness of the hospital.

'I'll be swimming down at the beach,' she told the bemused night sister.

Sister looked at her watch. 'Five-thirty,' she said morosely. 'You're mad. All of you!'

'All of us?'

'I reckon you'll be knocked over in the crowds down there,' the sister told her. 'Standing room only. Don't forget your water-wings, though. Lifesavers are a bit sparse at this hour.'

Sally gave a half-hearted attempt at a smile and let

herself out of the rear door. The sea lay below, a shimmering plane of glass in the dawn light, beckoning her as nothing else could.

Crowds?

Sally managed to smile as she looked along the deserted beach. There was no one, as far as the eye could see. She had the place to herself. This was why she had come to Gundowring, after all. The sea, sun, sand and Sally. Bother Lloyd Neale. He had no place here this morning.

It took seconds to pull her dress over her head, revealing an attractive white costume. Sally ran for the surf, revelling in the feel of soft sand through her toes. Maybe this way she could lessen the confusion that was making her exhausted.

She swam undisturbed for half an hour, letting the cool wash of the surf ease trouble from her mind. To a certain extent she was successful. The rhythm of the sea was a comfort—a reminder that she was insignificant in the scheme of things, and her troubles even less so. Finally she hauled herself out of the water on to a rocky shelf at the edge of the cove, let the early morning sun wash over her and drifted into a dreamless sleep.

She woke to find Lloyd Neale standing over her.

His shadow woke her. Lloyd's body was blocking the sun, and a steady rain of sea-water was splashing down from his gleaming body. Clearly he'd just emerged from the water. He stood looking down at the half-awake girl at his feet and his jaw dropped in astonishment.

'You!'

It was a breath of anger, and Sally held her hands up before her in a reflex action of defence.

'What. . .what are you doing here?' she whispered.

'I might say the same of you.' He gazed down at her as if he couldn't believe his eyes, and Sally realised that from the sea her sleeping body must have been out of sight. It was only when he'd pulled himself on to the ledge that he'd realised she was there.

'I'm sleeping,' she said defensively, her body cringing at his anger. 'It's not your ledge.'

'I always come here.'

'Well, if I'd known that I wouldn't have come.'

Sally struggled into a sitting position, excruciatingly aware of the scantiness of her swimming costume. Any remnant of sympathy from the night before was gone. The caring was part of a dream. Now. . . Lloyd Neale was obviously regretting any gesture he had made towards her, and his coldness hurt. It hurt more than any pain she had ever felt.

Sally hugged her arms across her breasts. The faint morning warmth had gone from the sun and she felt chilled to the bone. 'I wouldn't have dared encroach on the territory of the great Lloyd Neale,' she whispered up to him, fighting for armour against the pain. 'But I thought I had the cove to myself.'

The night sister's words came flooding back as she talked. 'You're mad. All of you!' This, then, was what she had meant. Lloyd also swam at dawn.

'It's not my territory,' he conceded. Lloyd hadn't moved. He stood, his legs slightly apart, his hands on his hips and his bare chest glinting wetly in the sun. He wore a brief bathing costume and nothing more, and Sally closed her eyes momentarily as she struggled to her feet. Heavens—how was she supposed to make herself impervious to this man?

'I'll go, nevertheless,' she managed, and turned to dive into the water. She was stopped by a hand gripping her arm. He swung her back to face him, brooking no protest.

'Sally, yesterday. . . We were both exhausted. Beyond reason.'

'And you didn't mean to kiss me,' Sally said flatly.

'So apologise and everything will be OK.' Like heck it would!

'I just wanted to comfort you. You seemed so upset.'

The sudden change of tone made Sally blink. He was shoving anger aside, searching for something civil to say. Sally opened her mouth to speak, but no words came out.

'You're not to blame yourself,' he continued harshly. 'You did everything you could to save the boy.'

'I'm not. . .I'm not blaming myself,' she whispered. 'But that kiss. . . That kiss wasn't for comfort.'

'I don't know what you read into it,' he said, and his voice was bleak, 'but I'm engaged, Sally. I intend to marry Margaret, and I'm asking you to forget it happened.'

'I've forgotten.' Her voice matched his for coldness.

'So why are you here?' Lloyd demanded. 'If you're not upset about the boy, and you've forgotten the kiss, you should be home, sleeping.'

'So should you.'

He was too darned close. Too close. . .

'The accident stirred me up as well,' Lloyd confessed. 'Stupid young kids. . .'

'It wasn't their fault.'

'They were fools.'

'Yeah.' Sally pulled back on her arm and he finally released her. She stood looking down at the white mark his hand had left. Mechanically she started rubbing it, as though her rubbing could dispel the remembrance of his touch. 'Idealistic kids, rushing to save the world. I seem to remember a story of Lloyd Neale doing exactly that.'

'And I learned,' he said bitterly. 'The hard way.'

'So you wouldn't rush in slaying dragons any more?' Sally asked slowly. She looked up at him, her clear hazel eyes challenging his denial. 'You've learned to take care of number one?'

'I've learned not to forgive stupidity,' he said harshly. 'I've seen what it can do.'

'And your answer is to condemn,' Sally whispered. 'That's a hard, hard judgement.'

'Yeah, well, you'll learn it in time, Dr Atchinson. It'll be a different story when stupidity affects something you hold precious. I'd like to see your notion of forgiveness then.'

Silence. Sally stood looking up at him. She was aware that the colour had drained from her face, and the summer sun had turned to ice. She gave an involuntary shudder. The memory of the night her father died flooded back with such clarity that she could feel the forces hauling her apart all over again. It was as much as she could do not to cry out.

'I'll. . .I'll leave you to your ledge,' she faltered.

Once more she turned to dive, but once more his hand came out to grip her. This time she didn't turn back, despite the force trying to turn her. She stood passive in his iron grip and looked away—out to sea—anywhere but into those all-seeing eyes.

'What did I say to make you look like that?'

'Nothing.' Sally's voice was so low he pulled her closer to hear. 'Nothing.'

Her whisper had a dangerous wobble and she fought for anger to defend herself—to stop the tears. 'You shouldn't have to ask, though, Dr Neale. You're so all-fired clever. You know all the answers. You know how to keep the world safe and dull and worthy. You and your precious Margaret. Now let me go. I don't want anything to do with you.'

'Sally. . .'

'No!'

It was a cry of pure pain. With a frantic pull, Sally managed to release herself from his clasp, and before he could move she stepped back and dived cleanly off the ledge—into the cool, clear depths below.

She had never dived so deep. She let her body sink further and further, until her lungs were screaming a protest, and then, reluctantly, she twisted her face to the sunlight and drifted up to the surface.

He was still on the ledge, silently watching. Sally emerged, spluttering, from the depths, cast one scared look up at his aloof, remote figure and struck out for shore. She didn't look back.

She couldn't. Her heart would break if she did.

It was only as she reached the beach and ran up the sand to her waiting clothes that she dared glimpse back.

He had dived off the ledge but he hadn't headed for shore. Lloyd Neale was swimming along the back of the line of surf running into the cove. His lithe, muscular body cut the water like a scythe. He might limp on land, but not here. He was a man in his element.

He wasn't enjoying himself, though. His head was down and he swam as if demons were following him. The demons of his past.

Damn Lloyd Neale.

Sally swore softly under her breath. She pulled her dress over her wet body and turned to the track away from the beach. That was the end of a perfect swim.

That was the end of her peace of mind.

CHAPTER SEVEN

THE rest of the day passed in a swirl of exhausted confusion. Somehow Sally managed to keep her mind on the job, but it was just as well that her surgical cases were routine. At the head of the table Lloyd administered anaesthetic for an appendicectomy with silent skill, and Sally had no idea what he was thinking.

'That's that, then,' she said finally, as she inspected her handiwork. 'I'm starting to close.'

'Don't hurry on my account,' Lloyd snapped. 'I await your pleasure.'

Sally gasped. The implication that she had been slow was obvious—but Sally knew that if she hadn't been painstakingly careful she would have risked her patient succumbing to peritonitis. She glared up at him, but Lloyd was concentrating on the monitors, his attention anywhere but on Sally.

You rude, arrogant, chauvinistic twit, she told him under her breath as she sewed up Mrs Crowe's appendicectomy. It was all she could do not to say the words out loud. I can't believe I let you kiss me. I can't believe I'm imagining myself in love with you.

She glanced up to the head of the table at Lloyd's grim face. He had been silent for the entire operation, concentrating on his patient and his monitors as if he were anaesthetising for open heart surgery instead of a routine appendicectomy.

If I keep on like this, I'll have to return to Melbourne, she thought sadly. She had known at the start that it would be impossible to work with an anaesthetist she didn't get on with—but an anaesthetist she had fallen in love with?

101

Crazy, crazy, crazy. Lloyd Neale was engaged to Margaret. He didn't like her. He thought she was silly and spoilt. . .

She couldn't keep going. She couldn't. She couldn't bear to stay here and watch him marry his Margaret and have worthy children and keep throwing his pointed little barbs at her. It would break her heart.

All this she decided in the time it took to suture the wound, but she knew she was right. There was no way she would get over Lloyd Neale—not while she worked with him every day and he watched her as if she were a. . .

'A flibbertigibbet,' she said out loud, and glared straight at him. She tied off the last thread with a flourish and deepened the glare.

'I beg your pardon?' His look didn't change, but the nurse behind Sally gave a nervous titter.

'That's what you think I am,' she said savagely. 'Reverse, please, Dr Neale.'

He raised his eyebrows sardonically and filled the syringe from the trolley at his side. 'I don't think anything of the kind.'

'That or worse.' She took a deep breath and managed to keep her voice even. 'Well, you've succeeded. I hope you're satisfied.'

'What the hell. . .?'

'Don't swear,' she snapped. Behind Sally, the nurse's jaw had dropped six inches. Nobody talked like this to Dr Neale!

'I'll swear if I want to,' Lloyd said, and to Sally's fury she saw a trace of laughter lurking behind his mask.

Sally's distress had reached the stage where something had to give. Her temper was barely containable. 'Oh, sure. You do anything you like, Dr Neale. You be as unbearable as you like to me, and don't give a damn about my feelings. No one in this town faces up to you. You think you're so damned special because you have a gammy leg. You're so virtuous. . . You give me the cold shoulder. You work with your mouth firmly shut and your eyes watching me every inch of the way—waiting for me to make a mistake. . .'

Sally swallowed. She desperately wanted to burst into tears and run, but her pride wouldn't let her.

'Well, you've been as rude as you possibly can to me over the last few weeks. You want me to leave this town and I guess you've now succeeded. It's months until the town's anaesthetist comes back, and I'd still have to work in the same town as you even then. Frankly, Dr Neale, I can't. Not now. Not ever. This town is too small. Come to think of it, this whole country's too small. So you've got your way. I agreed to work for a month and then see if I'd continue. A month takes me to next Friday. I'll leave then.'

She closed her eyes for one long moment, and then turned and walked out of the theatre.

You could have heard a pin drop behind her. The silence in the theatre was absolute.

He couldn't follow her. Lloyd still had an unconscious patient on his hands. Sally closed the theatre door behind her, stripped off her theatre gown and gloves, and walked slowly back to her apartment.

Finish.

That was that, then. End of a dream.

Was Gundowring the dream? Or Lloyd Neale?

Sally shook her head, trying to sort out her own feelings. Gundowring. . . Lloyd. . . The pain of leaving Gundowring would be enormous, but the pain of leaving Lloyd. . .

Pain. The raw ache that had been there since her father died was almost overwhelming.

Lloyd Neale didn't ask you to fall in love with him, Sally told herself. It's not his fault. So why have you fallen so hard when the man's such a bore? And engaged to someone else!

'I don't know!' She said the words out loud and it was almost a wail. She shoved the door of her apartment wide and stopped short.

Lisa Maitland was sitting in her big armchair.

'You're talking to yourself again,' the child told her.

Sally summoned a weak smile. 'I find I'm wittiest on my own.' She frowned down at the child with mock severity. 'And you're trespassing again. How did you get in?'

'Through the window,' Lisa confessed. 'Don't tell Dad.'

The turmoil in Sally's confused heart faded a little as she looked down at Lisa. 'You've been crying,' she said accusingly, and Lisa met her look.

'So have you.'

'I have not!' Sally gave a watery sniff. 'Grown-ups don't cry.'

'My Gina is.'

'Crying?'

'Yes.'

Sally dropped to her knees on the carpet and took Lisa's cold hands between hers. She could feel a tremor of fear running through the little girl's thin fingers.

'What's wrong, Lisa?'

'Our baby's sick.'

'Pumpkin?' Sally frowned. 'But she was fine yesterday.'

'I know. But this morning there was a bump on her tummy and Gina said it was a hernia. It got bigger this afternoon, and then Sarah started screaming and screaming and wouldn't stop—and Dad says it's a strangulating hernia, and he says we can't fix it here so the plane leaves in half an hour for Melbourne—and Dad says I have to stay with Margaret while they're away!'

The child's words ended on a wail and Lisa threw herself into Sally's arms and sobbed.

Sally's mind was racing as she held the sobbing child close. A strangulating hernia. . . Maybe. . .

'Lisa. . .' She took the child's shoulders in her hands and pushed her back from her. 'Lisa, I might be able to help. I'm a surgeon. I should be able to fix it.' She pulled a tissue from her pocket and gave it to Lisa, smiling faintly as the child blew her nose with the force of someone three times her age. 'Can you be brave and stay here while I go and find out? Are they in the children's ward?'

'Yes, But they said——'

'I know what they said,' Sally said softly. 'But maybe I can convince them otherwise.'

Sally left Lisa making herself a jam sandwich—sustenance for shock, Sally had advised—and made her way swiftly to the children's ward. The door swung open to reveal a group of four doctors clustered round a crib.

'Gina. . .' Sally crossed swiftly to the worried young mother and put her hand on her shoulder. 'Gina, what's going on?'

'It's Pumpkin. . .' Gina was no longer the competent young paediatrician. She was a scared young mum, and her fear was palpable. 'Her hernia's strangulating.'

Sally flicked back the covers on the crib and grimaced. There was no mistaking the signs. They were clear at a glance, and the child's thin wail of distress pierced everyone in the room.

'How long has it been like this?'

'An. . . An hour. Maybe a bit more. She seemed a little distressed this morning and I noticed the lump—but then she settled. She became really distressed just as you and Lloyd went into Theatre with Mrs Crowe's appendix.'

Sally winced. She looked down at the baby's tiny

abdomen and her fingers gently palpated the lump in the groin. 'So you tried to put it back yourself?' she guessed.

'Yes.' Gina looked up at Sally, her eyes bright with unshed tears. 'I knew you'd be better at it than me—but you were busy. . .'

Sally nodded. Gina had tried and failed, which would mean Sally had much less chance now of manipulating the bowel back into position without general anaesthetic.

'Will she go on to the breast?' Sally asked. For a tiny child like this, the best and safest method of pain relief seemed to be the mother's breast. It acted like a euphoric drug—more effective than any narcotic.

'She won't suckle any more,' Lloyd said grimly. 'Gina tried to shift the bowel while she fed—and it made the baby frantic.' His words were carefully non-critical, Gina had acted for the best—but it was so hard to act dispassionately when the screaming child was your own. If that first attempt at manipulation had been done with sure, steady fingers. . .

It couldn't be helped. The bowel had to be re-positioned. Now wasn't the time for recrimination. It was time for action.

'So why are you talking of sending her to Melbourne?' Sally asked. 'You know the risks of leaving the bowel strangulating for hours. Why not operate here?'

Silence.

'Look, it has to be fixed,' Sally said briefly. 'I know there are more experienced doctors in Melbourne—but I wouldn't offer to operate if I didn't think I could do it.'

The silence went on. Sally stared down at the baby and then back to Gina.

'Don't you trust me?' she asked Gina softly. 'Gina, I know I can do this.'

'Oh, I know.' With a watery gulp, Gina collected herself and threw an appealing glance at her husband. Struan, like Gina, white-faced and shaken, shook his head.

'Of course you can do it,' Struan said savagely. 'But Lloyd can't.'

'Lloyd. . .' Sally stared across at Lloyd. She'd been aware of his presence but it had been easy to ignore in the face of Gina and Struan's distress. Now his grim face flooded her thoughts.

'I'm not a qualified anaesthetist,' Lloyd said through gritted teeth. 'I saw Sarah an hour ago—before we did the appendicectomy. She was just starting to cry and Gina was worrying even then. I said then that if it strangulated I wasn't qualified to give the anaesthetic. I'm a physician, Sally. I've done my first part anaesthetics, but Sarah's three weeks old and needs real anaesthetic skill. They'll have to take the baby to Melbourne—fast.'

Sally closed her eyes for one long moment. When they opened again things were clearer to her. Lloyd's grim rudeness during the last operation. . . His hurry to be finished. . .

'Well, that's not your fault,' she said softly. 'You can't whip yourself because you're a physician and not an anaesthetist.'

'Can't he just?' Struan said grimly. 'Just watch him.'

'I have better things to do,' Sally said tightly. The look on Lloyd's face repelled her. Cold and bleak and hard. . .

Sally's fingers were still gently feeling the baby's groin. Her mind was racing. It was possible. . . She felt the hard bulge in the baby's groin once again. Maybe they could manage without a general anaesthetic.

'Lloyd, what about administering a relaxant? If we could make the little one stop straining then I might be able to manoeuvre it back into position.'

Lloyd stared, the thoughts behind his grim eyes a mystery. 'I can't administer an anaesthetic,' he said finally. 'But——'

'But I don't want a dead bowel when Sarah arrives in Melbourne,' Sally snapped. 'She's too little for a resection. So stop throwing me buts, Lloyd Neale. I'm not talking about an anaesthetic. I'm talking about a relaxant. Morphine? Pethidine? Maybe Phenergan would do it? For heaven's sake, Lloyd. . .'

He was with her. The sudden change in expression showed he understood. 'You think there's still a chance. . .'

'I've done it before. Never in such a little one—but my fingers are small and it's worth a try.'

He nodded. 'So all we need is a paediatrician to tell us a safe dosage.' Lloyd crossed to where Gina was staring helplessly down into the cradle.

'And I was forgetting,' he said gently. 'We have a paediatrician in our midst. Gina, love. . .'

Gine tore her face from her pain-racked child and looked piteously up at him.

'I can't bear it if anything happens to her, Lloyd.'

'No,' he said softly. He lifted her hands. 'But nothing will. For a moment, Gina, I want you to forget that Sarah is your baby. I want you to be our paediatrician, faced with a baby you want pain-free. A three-week-old, seven pound baby, Gina. Tell me the dosage. Can I use morphine, or will Phenergan do? Help me in this, Gina. You're the one who can help us now.'

'I. . .I can't think. . .'

'Then I'll have to ring Melbourne and ask, but you're on hand. A paediatrician on the other end of the telephone can't assess our Pumpkin. You can see how weak Sarah is, and you're an expert. So block out everything else and concentrate. For the moment,

Sarah is your patient—not your daughter. Can you do this, Gina?'

Sally watched, mesmerised. Gina's tear-drenched eyes came up to Lloyd's, then fell again to her baby daughter. She took an audible breath and then another.

'I guess. . .I guess. . .'

'I don't want a guess,' Lloyd said sharply. 'I want accurate dosage, Gina, and nothing else. If you can't be professional, then go and wait in Reception and leave this to us.'

'Leave her. . .'

'Help her or leave her.' Lloyd's voice was a douche of cold water and it produced miracles.

Gina's face set. She glanced from her husband to her baby, and then back to Lloyd.

'She's been in distress for over an hour.' She faltered, her voice firming as she spoke. 'And I hurt her. The shock. . .the shock will be taking effect. It shouldn't take much. I think. . .'

'Don't think!' Lloyd snapped. 'Know!'

'OK.' Gina's voice was becoming more detached as Lloyd's brutal methods worked. 'We should use four milligrams of pethidine. Given her condition, that's all that's safe. We can administer more later, if necessary.'

'Four milligrams. . .'

'Yes.'

'You're not going for a lesser dose because she's your daughter?'

'No.' Gina's eyes sparked a little. 'That's the dose, Lloyd.'

'Great.' His wide, encompassing smile lit the room and he gave Gina a swift hug. 'Now it's up to Sally and I. Let's go. Sister, you heard. I want a syringe here now. I want the plane delayed for half an hour to give us a chance. I want Dr Atchinson to have every opportunity of getting that bowel back into position for the journey.'

Half an hour later the tortured bowel slid back into the cavity from where it had come. Under Lloyd's watchful eyes, Pumpkin lay limp and silent, her huge eyes gazing up at the doctors above her.

The pethidine had worked miracles. The wails had died to nothing, allowing the bowel to relax and Sally's nimble fingers to ease it gently back into position. She sighed with relief as she saw it go, and then glanced up to see Lloyd's face break into a triumphant grin.

'Well done,' he said softly, and Sally felt a rush of colour to her face at the gentleness of his words.

Her impressions of this man as a chameleon were right, she thought grimly. There was a Lloyd Neale she hated—the Lloyd Neale who was frightened of life and who rejected her as a frivolous fool— and a Lloyd Neale who she had given her heart to— forever.

Lloyd had bullied this baby's frightened mother unmercifully, but it had worked. For those few crucial minutes, Gina had found the strength to think clearly, and Sally knew that it was solely thanks to Lloyd that the angry twisted bowel was safely back in position.

'For how long, though?' she whispered.

'God knows,' Lloyd said frankly, following her thoughts. 'But even if it twists again as the aeroplane takes off, at least the children's surgeon will be dealing with bowel that's been twisted for three hours rather than five. It's the best we can do, Sally.'

His voice softened as he spoke and Sally's eyes flew up to him. Chameleon. . .

'Let's go and tell Pumpkin's parents the good news, shall we?' he said, and before she knew it Lloyd's hand came out and took hers in his. Leaving Pumpkin in the charge sister's care, they walked out of Theatre together, their hands linked.

They were met by Gina and Struan and Lisa—and Margaret.

If looks could have killed, Sally would have fallen down dead on the spot. As it was, she tried to withdraw her hand from Lloyd's clasp as Margaret's eyes flashed fire, but Lloyd's hand only tightened. He raised her hand with his, in the gesture of announcing the winner of a prize fight.

'It's back.' He grinned. 'The bowel's slipped back into position, thanks to our surgeon extraordinaire. You can take you daughter safely to Melbourne, Gina and Struan. With any luck at all, she'll sleep all the way, and the surgeon in Melbourne will wonder what the fuss was about.'

'Why are you holding Sally's hand?'

The question came from Lisa, and Sally flushed bright crimson and tried to draw away. Lloyd, however, was having none of it.

'Because this lady has just done a tricky piece of manoeuvring and has succeeded.' He cast a glance at Margaret and grinned placatingly. 'If I wasn't affianced to my Margaret, I'd kiss her. . .' Finally he did let Sally go, limped across and took Margaret's hands. 'I'll just have to kiss my fiancée instead.'

'She's sure a poor alternative to Sally,' Lisa said scornfully, and was silenced by a look from her father. He was too worried, though, to give her rudeness the attention it deserved.

'Lisa, love, we still have to take Sarah to Melbourne,' Struan said worriedly. 'But Margaret's assured us she's happy to look after you. If things go well, I'll be back tomorrow, and Gina will return as soon as Sarah's able to travel.'

'I'm coming with you,' Lisa said stubbornly, only the wobble of her chin betraying her fear.

'Honey, you can't.' Struan pushed a hassled hand through his hair in a gesture of pure weariness. 'We'll have to stay in the children's hospital. There isn't accommodation for brothers and sisters—I've been hard put to it to organise accommodation for Gina and I. And I'll be back soon.'

'But I don't want to stay with Margaret.'

'Oh, for heaven's sake. . .' Margaret expostulated. She had pushed Lloyd away from her with a gesture of distaste at his public show of affection. Now she held out her hand in a school-marm's signal of desired obedience. 'Come with me, young lady, and stop making a fuss. Gina and Struan have enough to worry about without you behaving like a spoiled brat.'

'No. . .' The word came from both parents, and Lloyd cast Margaret a look of incredulity.

'For heaven's sake, Margaret. . .'

'Well, Sarah's their own wee daughter. It stands to reason they have to put her first.'

'Sarah's our second daughter,' Gina snapped, and gathered her first daughter close. 'Struan, we have to take Lisa.' The message was unspoken, but clear for all that. We can't leave her with this woman. She has to come. Lisa disappeared in her mother's embrace and her small shoulders heaved.

'Lisa, how about coming and staying with me?' Sally spoke softly.

She walked across to mother and daughter and laid her hand on Lisa's ruffled hair. Lisa didn't stir from Gina's embrace and her face was buried in Gina's breast.

'Lisa, the trip to Melbourne's going to be uncomfortable and hard. Your mum and dad aren't going to be able to look after you, and there'll be nothing for you to do in Melbourne while you're waiting for Pumpkin's operation. And you know I'd love to have you. Your mum's been telling me you know how to cook pancakes. If you stay with me, I'll insist on pancakes for breakfast—maybe even for supper tonight.'

There was a moment of silence. Finally, the shoulders gave a last heave and Lisa turned tear-stained eyes to Sally. 'R-really?'

'Really.' Sally smiled. 'And you've already lived in my flat, when you were little, so you'll feel at home.'

Lisa considered. 'I'd have to bring my dog,' she announced, and Struan groaned.

'Wacky's quite capable of caring for himself for twenty-four hours.'

'He gets lonely,' Lisa protested. 'And he's house-trained, Sally.'

'You mean, he's trained to sleep on your bed,' Gina laughed. 'Oh, Sally. . .'

'Gina, a dog is just what I need at the moment,' Sally assured Lisa's worried mother. 'I'm sure there's a mouse in my kitchen. I opened a whole packet of chocolate biscuits last night and this morning there were only two left. Now, you must realise I can't possibly have eaten all of them—even if I was watching a soppy movie on television. Therefore there has to be a mouse. How's Wacky at mouse-chasing?'

'Great!' Lisa pronounced. 'At least. . .' She cast a doubtful glance at her father and forced herself to be honest. 'If the mouse was a slow one. . .'

'Well, that's settled,' Sally said, satisfied. 'After half a packet of chocolate biscuits, our mouse won't be able to get past a waddle. Now, let's find your pyjamas while your dad packs for Melbourne.'

'But the child's staying with me.'

It was a hard, flat statement, and Sally turned to see fury flash again from Margaret's eyes.

'Oh, for heaven's sake. . .' Lloyd seemed as angry as Margaret, but for different reasons. 'Margaret, Lisa can't stay with you. Can't you see how you've hurt her?'

Margaret's face went white. She put a hand up to blanched cheeks and stared at Lloyd. 'Hurt. . . I didn't mean. . . I wanted her to stay. Really, Lloyd. . .'

'I know you did. . .' His voice softened. 'But she'll be happier with Sally.'

'Because Sally will indulge her with every stupid whim. Spoil her rotten.' Margaret's voice was rising on a note of hysteria. 'Sally's nothing but trouble. You said that yourself, Lloyd. She flaunts herself all over the town and you. . .you fall for it. Holding hands with a woman who's no more than a hussy. . .'

'Margaret!'

Lloyd's sharp voice cut across Margaret's outburst. Around them, the rest of the group looked just plain horrified.

'Well, she is.' Margaret's words dropped to a sullen whisper. 'How can you agree to let her have the child when you agreed with me that she's an irresponsible tart?'

'I did no such thing. . .'

'Oh, for heaven's sake. . .' Sally took a deep breath and struggled to decide whether to laugh or cry. One look at Lloyd's grim face, however, threw laughter aside, and she was darned if she was going to cry. So Lloyd had been sharing his feelings with his beloved. . .

'Margaret, you won't have to fear my corrupting presence much longer,' Sally said slowly. 'What you and Lloyd think of me has been apparent from the start. I intend to take good care of Lisa—if it's OK with her parents—but after that. . . Well, I'm finishing up here at the end of the month.'

Margaret's breath drew in on a frightened hiss. Her jaw dropped open—as though she doubted her own powers.

'You're lying,' she spat.

'A liar as well as a slut. . .' Sally shook her head. 'I don't know what I've done to deserve this, Margaret. I can only ignore it.' She turned to Gina. 'Gina, do you trust me with Lisa while you're away?'

'Of course I do.' Gina was close to tears. 'Sally, you can't leave. Of all the vindictive. . .'

'It's not me being vindictive——' Margaret started, but Lloyd shook his head, his hand coming out to her arm and his eyes effectively silencing her.

'We'll talk this through later.' Lloyd's voice was laced with suppressed fury, whether at Sally or Margaret Sally couldn't tell. His cold face said that the matter, as far as he was concerned, was closed. Margaret had no choice but to bite her lip and turn her mortified face away.

'We have to get this baby organised for the flight,' Lloyd continued. 'It seems to me, young Lisa, that you should have chosen Margaret to stay with after all. With Struan and Gina both away this hospital is going to be dangerously short-handed. You might find yourself more of a dogsbody than Wacky.'

'I don't mind working for Sally,' Lisa said stoutly. She cast a defiant look at Margaret. 'She makes me laugh.'

'There'll be no time for laughing in the next few days,' Lloyd said solemnly, ignoring the flushed, mortified face of his fiancée beside him. 'We'll be lucky if there's enough time to breathe!'

The first few hours, at least, weren't a rush. Sally had time to settle Lisa into the flat, do a peaceful ward-round and come back to enjoy a leisurely dinner with her new charge. Afterwards they made pancakes, a messy business which all enjoyed—even Wacky, the boisterous Labrador who had arrived with Lisa's suitcase.

'Yum,' Lisa said sleepily as she licked her fingers

free of the last of the maple syrup. 'Four pancakes! I'll be fatter than your mouse.'

'And Wacky's eaten six.' Sally smiled. 'He's in no condition to mouse-chase now. Bed for you both, young Lisa.'

Lisa protested, but feebly. The emotions of the day had left her exhausted. Sally tucked her into the spare bed, Wacky beside her, and kissed her goodnight.

'You weren't serious about leaving Gundowring?' Lisa asked as she faded towards sleep. 'You don't really want to leave us?'

Sally stood and looked down at the child's anxious face. Not tonight. She couldn't tell her tonight.

'No, Lisa,' she said softly. 'I don't really want to leave you.' She placed a kiss on the child's cheek and walked softly back out into the living-room.

Mess! Pancake batter spread from end to end. Sally had been called back to the ward just as Lisa and Wacky had discovered the electric beaters, and the results were a disaster.

'Uuugh. . .'

'You called?'

Sally spun round. She'd left the door from her living-room through to the hospital corridor unlocked, and Lloyd Neale was standing framed within the open doorway.

'You. . .'

'That's not very welcoming.'

Sally bit her lip and turned back to the sink. 'It wasn't meant to be. Go away.'

'Don't you want to know how Pumpkin got on?'

Sally dropped her dishcloth and turned involuntarily. Her eyes flew to Lloyd's. 'Oh, Lloyd. . .'

'She's fine.' Lloyd saw the momentary panic flare behind Sally's eyes and was swift to reassure her. He limped across to pick up her dishcloth. 'The bowel stayed in place until she arrived at the children's hospital. They operated straight away as they were worried about the damage done by the previous torsion—but she's fine. All repaired. Two relieved parents and one healthy baby.'

'Oh, that's lovely. I'll tell Lisa. . .'

Lisa, though, was in no condition to be told. She was as soundly asleep as only a healthy child could be—earthquakes couldn't have woken her.

'I guess at least she's not lying there worrying,' Sally said doubtfully.

'Children don't. They assume the best, until the best has proved impossible.'

'Lucky them.'

'Sally. . .'

'Look, there's really nothing I need to say to you,' Sally said desperately. 'I don't want you here.'

'I don't want you to leave Gundowring.'

Silence. They stood staring at each other across the width of the room. Lloyd was holding his stick in one hand, the dishcloth in the other. He looked uncertain, as if he had no idea of why he was really there.

'I think you do,' Sally said gently. 'I think you don't want me here, Lloyd Neale. I think I unsettle you as much as you unsettle me—and you sure as heck unsettle me.'

'What are you saying?'

Sally took a deep breath. There was nothing to lose now. Only pride, and she had never been much for pride. An empty, futile emotion, especially if it prevented her from fighting for the only thing in the world she held dear.

'I'm saying I've fallen in love with you, damn you,' she said softly. 'You can do with it what you like. It seems to me that you don't want anything at all to do with it, but that hasn't stopped me from falling in love with you.'

'No.'

A douche of ice-water couldn't have felt as bad. Lloyd's single word hit Sally in the face and she recoiled as if slapped.

'Well. . .' Sally turned away to the sink, fighting tears. 'It doesn't matter. I just thought you ought to know, that's all.'

'You don't fall in love like that.'

He hadn't moved. He stood motionless, and his voice was carefully devoid of emotion. 'What we're feeling. . .'

'We?'

'We, dammit!' He moved then, limping swiftly across the kitchenette to grasp her by the shoulders. 'You think I can't feel this thing between us? This. . . This animal attraction. . .'

'Animal attraction! Between noble physician and Gundowring's latest tart!'

'I didn't call you that.'

'Margaret said you did.'

'Sally, I didn't. I wouldn't.'

'Then stop treating me as one.' Sally gave in to the insistent pull on her shoulers and whirled to face him. 'You treat me as less than worthless. You treat me as if I'm trying to corrupt you—as though it was me forcing you to kiss me yesterday. You apologised for losing control. How on earth do you think that makes me feel?'

'I haven't a clue.' He was so darned close it was a physical hurt to have him there, and it was all Sally could do to make herself listen to his words. 'I only know that this thing between us—this. . .this force. . .is cheapening both of us.'

'And what you have with Margaret is much more worthy?'

'She's a sensible girl. She's not——'

'She's not going to let her emotions run away with her. No.' Sally hauled his hands off her shoulders and turned away. 'I can see that. Well, I hope you'll be very happy, Lloyd Neale. I just don't want to stick around and watch.'

'That's nonsense.'

'What's nonsense?'

'To leave because you think you're in love with me.'

'But I'm flighty,' Sally said bitterly, squeezing liquid soap into the sink, turning the tap on full and regarding the gush of water with grim satisfaction. 'Surely you can't expect anything else of someone with her head full of fluff? Ruled by her emotions, that's me.'

'Sally. . .'

Once more the hands came down on her shoulders. Once more she was swung around to face his grim, intent look.

'Sally, this love thing——' He stopped and closed his eyes momentarily. 'It's not something for instant impulse. . . For emotion. . .'

'You mean emotion doesn't come into love?' Sally shook her head. 'That's crazy.'

'Of course it does. I couldn't marry Margaret if I wasn't emotionally attracted to her.'

'Well, bully for you,' Sally whispered. 'Off you go and marry her, then.'

'And you'll still leave Gundowring?'

'Yes, I will!' Untended, the water splashed up over the sink and on to the floor. Sally swore, spun around and twisted the tap off. It didn't quite stop running, but she didn't notice. 'If not because of you, then because of your precious Margaret. She thinks I'm a slut and I've never had anyone think that of me—much less tell me to my face.'

'If she apologises, will you stay?'

'No!'

'Then you're behaving like a child.'

'Sure.' Sally gazed down at the mess on the floor.

Soap-suds had cascaded down on to spilt batter. It all seemed too darned much.

'Go away,' she said slowly. 'Please, Lloyd. I've had enough.'

'I'll help you clean up.'

'I don't want your help,' she whispered. 'I don't want anything else at all. Not from you. Not now. Not ever.'

There was a long silence, broken only by the steady drip of water from bench-top to floor. Nothing.

'You'll see that I'm right eventually,' Lloyd said heavily. 'One day, Sally, you'll learn that following emotions is dangerous. Stupid. One day you'll be hurt, too. Life's not always as pleasant as yours has been so far.'

'You know nothing about my life.'

'I know you live in a soap bubble,' he said. 'You don't take life seriously.'

'Well, leave me to my soap bubble!' Sally stamped her foot, showering them both with a spray of soapy water. 'Get out of my apartment, Lloyd Neale. Get out now, or I'll scream this hospital down. I'll call the police and have you dragged out. Get out. Get out. Get out!'

'You'll stay?'

'I will not stay in this place one moment longer than I have to,' she yelled. Dignity, as well as pride, were things of the past, and she didn't care at all. She slopped across the room with sodden feet and hauled the door open. 'Just get out and stay out. I'll operate with you to the end of the week and then I'll be happy if I never see you again in my life!'

CHAPTER EIGHT

'SALLY.'

Sally woke with a jolt. Her bedside clock said one a.m. and she'd somehow hauled the telephone receiver down on to the pillow. Now Lloyd's voice came through as clearly as if he was in bed beside her.

'What the. . .?'

'Do you have the floor clean yet?'

She was wide awake now. Fumbling with the bedside light, Sally sat up in bed and glared at the telephone.

'Is that all. . .?'

'Don't hang up.' His voice was suddenly urgent and professional. Personal issues aside, his voice was saying.

'What's wrong?'

He sighed, and she could hear the relief that she wasn't going to let her personal feelings intrude on work. 'Sally, I've just done a house-call on Lorna Dalziel. She's in real trouble. I'm ringing you from her home before we ambulance her in.'

'Lorna. . .' Sally clicked back through half-forgotten advice. 'Isn't she the Munchausen case?' She remembered Lloyd talking of Lorna the first day they met.

'She is,' Lloyd said grimly. 'And she's darn near died of it.'

'I beg your pardon?' Sally stared blankly at the phone. Munchausen's syndrome was the imagination of every conceivable ill. No one had died of it yet.

'She's been complaining of chest pains for days,' Lloyd said grimly. 'Well, years, really, along with everything else, but for the past few days the favoured

symptoms have been chest pains again. She wept on
Gerard, her family doctor, this morning, but he was
frantically busy and didn't give her the time of day.
To give him his due, he's performed a dozen ECG
tests on Lorna over the past twelve months—and
referred her to me. We found nothing. So this afternoon she went home to bed, then rang me half an
hour ago to say if we didn't do something soon she
was going to die.'

'And?'

'And I'm a sucker for Lorna,' Lloyd admitted. 'And,
well. . . To be honest, she sounded scared. For once
she wasn't aggressive. Just in pain and fear. So I did
a house-call. After being bitten twice on the ankle by
her stupid Pekinese, I managed to examine her. She
has a ruptured aneurysm.'

'A ruptured——' Sally's mind flew into top gear. A
bursting of the main artery leading from the heart.
'Oh, no. . .'

'Sally, she won't live to get to the city. The ambulance has arrived, I've put on a pressure vest and I
have her comfortable, but she's bleeding to death
internally. We operate or she dies.'

'But we can't do that sort of operation here.'

'Yes, we can,' Lloyd said harshly. 'We must. We
operate, and she might die. We don't operate, and she
will die. So scrub, Sally. We're bringing her in now.'

The next few minutes passed in a haze. Somehow
Sally managed to dress, ask one of the nurses to keep
an eye on the sleeping Lisa, and organise Theatre. By
the time Lloyd arrived with their patient, Sally was
checking through theatre trays and going over and over
procedures in her head. This sort of operation was
one done by the senior surgeons in the big teaching
hospitals. Even then there was a huge chance of the
patient dying.

She mustn't let her doubts show. Lorna was sleepy

but awake as she was wheeled through into Theatre, and Sally smiled down into her frightened eyes.

'Well, Mrs Dalziel. You have a problem you want us to fix?'

'I. . .I told them I had chest pain,' Lorna Dalziel said weakly. 'They wouldn't believe me.'

Sally looked up to find laughter in Lloyd's grey eyes. If Lorna Dalziel died, his look told her, she'd die with 'I told you so' on her lips. A woman who had died happy.

Not if Sally could help it. She checked Lorna's pulse and winced. Lloyd was already attaching monitors.

'We're going to need another doctor,' Sally muttered. Major surgery such as this with only one anaesthetist and one surgeon was out of the question. Especially when the assisting nurses hadn't been trained to this sort of surgery.

'Gerard's on his way,' Lloyd told her. 'He's feeling pretty bad about this.'

'And so he should be,' Lorna said stoutly. 'He never takes me seriously. Only last week I told him I was sure I'd caught malaria from two backpackers who came through the town last month—and he refused to give me a blood test! Well, I told my daughter, Mandy, before I came in, "If anything happens to me then you sue the bastards. Sue the lot of them."' She glanced up at Lloyd. 'And you. . . You needn't think you're giving me an anaesthetic. You're not qualified. You can just take me to Melbourne and I'll have my operation there.'

Sally glanced up at Lloyd's face and then took Lorna's hand. 'Mrs Dalziel, do you know what's wrong?'

'He told me I had a hole in one of my arteries.' Fear was trickling through her words. Fear and defiance. 'But if he thinks he can use me as a training pigeon. . .'

'Mrs Dalziel, Dr Neale's our only anaesthetist. We haven't time to send you to Melbourne. You have to agree to Lloyd giving you the anaesthetic.'

'Or I'll die?'

Once more Sally glanced at Lloyd. His face was unreadable. 'Yes,' she said bluntly.

The lady's eyes widened.

'So you're not even giving me a choice?'

'There isn't one to give you,' Sally told her. 'I'm sorry. You can refuse the operation—but your blood pressure's way down already. Honestly, Mrs Dalziel. . .'

The woman stared up at her. What she read in Sally's eyes made her close her own eyes in fear. 'O-OK, then.' She looked across at the door, where her daughter was standing, frightened and silent. 'Only, if I die—you sue the pack of them,' she ordered her daughter. 'Sue 'em, Mandy. . . Sue them for not listening, and sue Dr Neale for not giving me a proper anaesthetic.' Then she sighed, and the fear faded a little from her eyes. 'Eh, I'm glad the pain's stopped. I'm so sleepy. . .'

Sally bit her lip and glanced up at Lloyd.

Now what?

Lloyd had now been threatened with a law-suit at the outset. It was true—he wasn't an anaesthetist. With the threat of a law-suit already hanging over his head, would he want to send the dying Lorna to Melbourne?

He wouldn't. She knew he wouldn't.

Lloyd signalled Sally with his eyes. Sally nodded, and Lloyd's hand moved. There was seemingly no decision on his part. His syringe went home in the back of Lorna's hand and she slid into oblivion.

The procedure was tricky. Sally made a long, mid-line abdominal incision and all of a sudden there was blood everywhere. Gerard was behind her, suctioning off blood, but it flooded back faster than he could suction. To expose the aneurysm and stop the bleeding was often the trickiest part of the whole darned operation.

If she could just get this mess clear—see what she was doing. Gerard carefully positioned the sucker, clearing the oozing blood, and for a moment Sally saw what she was looking for—praying for. A neat split. . . The blood oozed through and hid it from view again, but now she knew what she was up against.

Two minutes later the clamps were in position. There. . . The pumping blood ceased like magic.

How much blood had she lost? Sally flicked a look up at Lloyd's grim face. This time his grimness wasn't because he was preoccupied or annoyed with his surgeon. This operation would take every ounce of Lloyd's skill.

All eyes were on Sally's fingers—except for Lloyd's. With the patient's blood pressure down so low before surgery even began, it was up to Lloyd to keep her alive.

People made such a fuss about choosing their surgeon, Sally thought appreciatively, glancing up to ask a silent message of Lloyd and having her answer back by the same route. But a skilled anaesthetist was often more important than the surgeon—especially now.

And Lloyd wasn't an anaesthetist. He'd done his first part, but now. . . He should be refusing to perform this as beyond his scope.

That he hadn't done so took Sally's breath away. He was prepared to take a risk, then—when life was at stake.

He was setting up more blood. Lorna could well have used eight or ten units of blood before the end of this. It was just as well she was a common blood group.

It was just as well that Lloyd Neale was a skilled anaesthetist.

Time and time again over the next hours Sally
blessed her small fingers. How on earth did surgeons
with big hands manage? she wondered. They'd have
to depend more on their tools, she knew, but her
fingers were dextrous enough to perform all but the
most intricate manoeuvre.

To repair the aneurysm she had to use a graft. If
Sally had been operating in one of the larger hospitals
she'd have called for advice on how to fit the dacron
graft for use. She'd seen this done—but always as a
student.

If she'd been in a large hospital she wouldn't be
doing this operation, for heaven's sake. This was senior
surgeon territory. As it was, she guessed she was lucky
that at least the hospital had some of the woven tubular
graft on hand.

And maybe it was enough. . .

You're on your own, she told herself firmly, and
then glanced fleetingly up at Lloyd. Like Sally, this
was a job he'd prefer someone else to be doing.

Sally and Lloyd. . . Or no one. And she wasn't on
her own. She was with Lloyd.

Their eyes met for a fraction of a second. It was
enough. The doubts subsided. Sally took a deep breath
and her nimble fingers kept moving.

'I think that's it,' she said finally, glancing up at
Lloyd's face. His eyes hadn't seen what she had been
doing. They had been moving from Lorna's face to
the dials beside him and back to Lorna's face like a
watchful hawk for more than two hours now. Heaven
knew how he had kept her alive during Sally's work,
but Sally knew that Lorna's chance at life was more
due to Lloyd's skill than hers.

And Lloyd's willingness to lay his neck on the line.

If he failed. . . If he failed, then Sally knew exactly
the scenario that would ensue. She'd seen the daughter's face as she had soaked in the mother's threat,

and she'd seen the hint of hope behind Mandy's eyes.
There was a mercenary streak in Mandy Dalziel—she
didn't need to be told that. If Lorna died, then Mandy
would stand in court and say her mother had refused
to let an unqualified anaesthetist near her—and that
Lloyd had persisted. They'd probably find someone,
somewhere to say Lorna would have lived until she
arrived in Melbourne. It was easy to be wise after
the event.

'I think we might have done it,' she said softly,
finally, as the clamps were removed and she checked
and checked again for inner bleeds. Finally she began
closing the abdomen. This in itself would take time.
Her fingers flew, however. The sooner they had Lorna
out of anaesthetic, the better.

'That's some skill,' Lloyd muttered, his eyes still on
his dials. 'I thought we'd lost her for sure.'

She flashed him a look. 'And yet you agreed to gas?
I thought you were afraid of dragons, Dr Neale.'

'Only one dragon,' he said, so softly that Sally
thought she must have misheard. 'Only one dragon.'

Afterwards, Sally cleaned herself and then went out
to talk to Mandy. She hadn't imagined the mercenary
streak. There was a look of disappointment, swiftly
suppressed, as Sally told her that her mother might
well live. It was far too early to be sure—but the
operation itself had been successful.

Poor Lorna. Maybe this was why she had
Munchausen's—if her family were as cold as this
daughter.

'It's early days yet,' she told Mandy. 'She'll be in
Intensive Care for a few days. I wouldn't abandon all
hope of law-suits.'

The girl's eyes flashed up to hers, and she had the
grace to blush. 'I wouldn't. . . I never. . . It was only
that Mum said. . .'

'I know what your mother said,' Sally said quietly. 'But maybe. . . Maybe it's not great tactics to put an axe like that over a doctor's head before he's about to start operating.'

'It doesn't matter,' the girl said sullenly. 'All you doctors have insurance.'

'And we have reputations,' Sally told her. 'A successful law-suit, no matter how unfair, can damage a doctor's livelihood forever. Dr Neale was your mother's only hope of survival, and by threatening him with legal action you caused him to think twice about giving the anaesthetic. Do you really want your mother to die?'

'Of. . .of course not.'

Only if it meant lots of money, Sally thought grimly, but she didn't say it. She turned away in disgust, to find Lloyd watching her from the door.

'You can see your mother now,' he told Mandy. 'She's barely conscious, so don't try to talk.'

'There's no point me seeing her then, is there?' Mandy sniffed. 'I'm off home. I'm so tired I can hardly think straight.' She walked out, banging the door behind her.

'Whew. . .'

'She's a cold fish, all right,' Lloyd agreed. He stood beside the door and watched Sally's face. 'That was a fine piece of surgery, Sally. We'll be the poorer in Gundowring without you. Please. . . I'd like you to reconsider your decision to leave.'

Sally's eyes flew up to his. 'I. . .I can't.'

'Your reasons for leaving are stupid.'

'Emotional. Not stupid.'

'But not insurmountable.'

'They are.' Sally closed her eyes, fatigue washing over her in waves. Intense surgery like that—it was like running a marathon. 'Look, Lloyd, even if I could find some way of dealing with my feelings. . . Margaret knows. She's not a fool. Why do you think she hates me?'

'She doesn't hate you.'

'No?'

'No.' He stood, irresolute. His hands came up and then fell away at his sides, as if he were making a superhuman effort not to touch her. 'Look, Sally, if I could make you see that these things can be overcome. If Margaret came and saw you. . . Apologised. . .'

'That would be just dandy.' Sally turned away to hide her face. 'Lloyd, I'm too tired to think now. Can we talk about it in the morning?'

'You will think about it, though?' he asked.

'Oh, I'll think,' Sally said bitterly. 'I've a whole three hours left of tonight. Hours and hours for all the thinking in the world.'

Despite her intention and need to sleep, Sally indeed spent most of the next three hours thinking. She dozed off at last through sheer exhaustion, but woke to find Lisa and Wacky bouncing on the foot of her bed.

'You don't have Vegemite,' Lisa said scornfully. 'What sort of place is this—with no Vegemite?'

'What's wrong with honey, you horrible child?' Sally pulled her pillow over her head. 'Go away.'

'It'll have to do,' Lisa sniffed. 'But Wacky likes Vegemite. He'll probably sulk.'

It didn't seem to affect him too deeply. By the time Sally was showered and dressed, Lisa and Wacky were rolling on the hospital lawns outside Sally's windows. Sally poured herself coffee as she watched them, thanking her stars that today was Saturday and she wasn't consulting. She could have half an hour at least before she needed to do her ward-rounds.

A knock on the door broke the stillness and Sally jumped. Drat, she was as nervous as a kitten. Lack of sleep, she told herself crossly as she crossed to open the door.

Margaret was on the other side, rigid with resolution.

'M-Margaret. . .' Sally stood aside, her heart sinking at the sight of her visitor. 'Come in.'

'I expect you know why I'm here,' Margaret said coldly, coming through into the flat and looking around.

'No.' Sally took a deep breath. 'I don't.'

'Lloyd told me I had to apologise.'

'That was big of Lloyd.'

Margaret stared at her, and to Sally's dismay she saw tears well in the woman's eyes and start to fall.

Oh, help. . . Now what?

'Come and have a coffee,' Sally said, her voice gentling. 'Have you had breakfast?'

'Yes. . . No. . . I don't want any.' The woman stood in the centre of the living-room and fought for composure. She lost it. Her hands came up to hide her eyes and her shoulders heaved. 'Oh, damn. . . I don't. . .'

'You don't cry?'

'No, I don't.' Margaret's eyes flew open and she looked beseechingly at Sally. 'It's just. . . Lloyd says I've been behaving appallingly, and it's true. I have. But it's not fair. Why do they just look at you. . .? I didn't mind the way Lloyd looked at you so much. But Randolph, too. It's not fair.'

'Randolph?' Sally had turned away to pour coffee, trying to give Margaret time to pull herself together. Now she turned back and stared. 'Randolph?'

'He's my second cousin,' Margaret whispered. 'And we were going to get married. Only, then. . . My mother told us about my great-grandfather. He was Randolph's great-grandfather as well. He died when he was in his early thirties because he had haemophilia. My mother said it'd be sinful for Randolph and I to get married. We'd be twice as likely to carry the disease. So we decided not to—and then I met Lloyd and I knew I could help him. I'd be good for him. But he looks at you like. . . And now. . . And now Randolph looks at you in the same way!'

Her last words went up on a rising note of hysteria. She buried her face in her hands once again and succumbed to sobs.

'Oh, my dear. . .'

Sally's gentle heart wrenched, her intuitive dislike of the woman put aside at Margaret's obvious distress. She crossed to take Margaret's hands, pulling them down from her eyes, and then gently led her across to the settee.

'Now, Margaret,' she said, trying to keep her voice dispassionate and professional. Her cool, calm, counselling best. 'Would you like to tell me all this from the beginning?'

Ten minutes later, Sally was staring at the other woman in bemusement.

'You mean. . . You mean, you and Randolph broke off your engagement without any sort of genetic counselling?'

'We read books,' Margaret said miserably. 'Everything said we shouldn't marry.'

'But you can be tested.'

'Tested?'

'Tested,' Sally said softly, looking down into Margaret's miserable face. Any trace of vindictiveness had gone from Margaret. Margaret looked desperately in earnest and desperately unhappy.

'It shouldn't matter,' Margaret said. 'I mean. . .I want children, and so does Randolph—so if we can't bear them. . . And Lloyd. . . Lloyd's a fine person. I know I can look after him and help him be someone worthwhile. I just about had it under control when you came—and Lloyd started looking at you like Randolph used to look at me. And then Randolph. . . At the dance. . .'

'Margaret, you're imagining things,' Sally told her a trifle breathlessly. 'Lloyd doesn't look at me like. . . He doesn't like me.'

'No.' A hint of the old Margaret waspishness returned. 'He doesn't like you. He just can't stop thinking about you. He can't stop talking about you, and I'm ready to throw something at him. He used to talk about the things I thought were important. And he agreed with me about things like. . .well, like child-rearing. Not now, though. He's changed, and it's your doing. And maybe I could bear it. . . But not if you have my Randolph.'

'Hey, Margaret, I have no intention of having "your" Randolph——' Sally started, but broke off at yet another knock on the door.

Some Saturday morning sleep-in, Sally thought ruefully. Lisa, Wacky, Margaret—and now who? She opened the door—to find Randolph Small standing on the other side.

'I was wondering whether you'd be free for a pic-nic——' he started, and then broke off as he saw who was with Sally. 'M-Margaret.'

It was too much for Margaret. She took one look at her ex-beloved and succumbed to a fresh paroxysm of weeping.

Oh, heck. . .

Things were way out of control. Sally took a breath, wondering whether she should tell Randolph to go away, but before she could do anything Randolph burst through the door and was at his cousin's side.

'Hey, Margaret. . . Honey, what's wrong?' He enfolded her in ample arms and looked help-lessly up at Sally. 'She's. . .she's my cousin, you know.'

'I know,' Sally said drily. She crossed to the kitchenette. 'I think I need a coffee, if no one else does.'

From within the circle of her cousin's arms, Margaret made a supreme effort. She thrust Randolph's arms away and rose unsteadily to her feet.

'I. . .I'm so sorry. Randolph, you mustn't. . .'

'I can comfort my own cousin when she's in trouble.' Randolph cast an almost defiant glance at Sally, and it was all Sally could do not to laugh. She put down the mug she had picked up and looked across at the not so cousinly couple.

'You can comfort your own love,' she said firmly.

Randolph visibly gulped. He looked helplessly at Sally and then down to the woman in his arms. 'What. . .? I don't. . . I mean, I came to ask you out.'

'But you love Margaret.'

'Yes. . . No. . . I mean, she's my cousin. . .'

'Second cousin, once removed on your father's side.' Sally smiled. 'Hardly kissing cousins. Yet you seem to be making a fair fist of it.'

Margaret took a gulping, sobbing breath and tried to push Randolph away. 'This. . . This is crazy. I shouldn't be here. Randolph. . .'

'Can I arrange an appointment for you two with a genetic counsellor?'

They both gaped at Sally. 'A. . .a what?' asked Randolph.

'A genetic counsellor. A doctor whose speciality is inherited disorders.' Sally's voice firmed at the look of incredulity on both faces before her. They were like a couple of scared kids. 'Do either of your parents suffer from haemophilia?' she asked.

'N-no,' Margaret quavered. 'But. . .'

'Your grandparents?'

'No.'

'So—let's see, then. Your great-grandfather died because he was haemophiliac. Before he died, he and his wife had your separate grandparents. Grandmothers or grandfathers?'

'Two. . .two boys. Our respective grandfathers. And then another girl.' Margaret gave a watery sniff.

Sally nodded. 'Well, I'm sure there are tests that can be done, but I think you might find you're clear. Girls tend to be the carriers and boys the sufferers. Chances are that if your grandfathers didn't have the disease then they didn't carry it on.'

'But. . .' Randolph was thinking things through. 'Our other cousin died from it. He descended from the girl in the same family. His grandmother was our grandfathers' sister.'

'And she had a daughter, who had you male cousin who died.' Sally nodded. 'It makes sense. Your grandfather's sister was a carrier. She passed the tendency to the disease to her daughter, who gave it to her son. It doesn't make it more likely that either of you are carriers.'

'But. . .'

'Look, I'm not a genetic counsellor,' Sally said firmly. 'I know very little more than you. But I do know that you shouldn't be making life decisions on the basis of superstitious fear. You need scientific fact.'

Randolph's face was slowly breaking into a grin. 'You mean. . .? You mean, Margy and I might be able to be married after all?'

'You might, at that. Would you like me to make an appointment with a genetic counsellor?'

'Yes, please.' His reply was so loud it brought the glimmer of a smile to Margaret's tearstained face.

'But. . .but what about Lloyd?' she whispered.

Sally hesitated, wicked suggestions whispering themselves into their inner ear. She fought them back with difficulty.

'Why don't you listen to what the genetic counsellor

says before you come to any decision,' she said gently. 'It's hardly fair on Randolph to do anything else.'

'That's right,' Randolph said ponderously. 'And if your mother was wrong, Margaret. . .' His chest swelled in indignation. 'Well, I know how to claim my own,' he proclaimed. 'In fact, I'm starting to think that whatever this damned genetic counsellor says we might take a chance. What happens if I find you crying again, Margy? I'm damned if I'll let some other man dry your tears. Lloyd Neale will just have to stand aside. A man's got to do what a man's got to do.'

It was all Sally could do not to choke with laughter. Instead she walked over to the door.

'Pistols at dawn?' She let a faint smile glimmer through. 'Make it something less messy, will you, Randolph? Or do it somewhere other than in my living-room. Now, if you'll excuse me. . .I haven't done a ward-round yet.'

She swung the door open and found Lloyd there, his hand poised, ready to knock.

'Oh, great. . .'

It was all Sally could do not to burst into hysterical laughter. She felt like it. The expressions on Randolph's and Margaret's faces were ludicrous—two children caught in crime. Randolph's arm didn't move from Margaret's waist, however.

'What the heck. . .?' Lloyd walked two paces into the living-room and stopped. 'What on earth is going on here?'

'I've just been doing a spot of matchmaking,' Sally said innocently. She choked. It was just all too much.

'What?'

Sometimes there was only one answer to an intolerable situation—the coward's way out.

'I'm sorry, Lloyd, but a girl's got to do what a girl's got to do,' she said solemnly, her voice an exact imitation of Randolph's earlier announcement. 'So,

if you'll excuse me, Lloyd. . . I've got to do a
ward-round.'

She took a deep breath, walked out, and closed the
door behind her.

CHAPTER NINE

SALLY did a purposely long ward-round, confident that if Lisa or Wacky needed her then they only had to search the hospital. From time to time she looked out into the hospital garden to see them rolling on the lawns. Minimal babysitting was required.

How soon could she return to the apartment? Not until the coast was likely to be clear, she decided. She'd stay away all day if she had to.

She couldn't stay away that long. She checked Lorna, who seemed, amazingly, to be holding her own, checked her other patients, had a long chat to Henry Butler and then looked out to see Lisa and Wacky return inside. The time had come to face the music.

Maybe they'd gone, leaving the apartment to herself and Lisa. There was no reason for Margaret, Randolph or Lloyd to stay.

So don't be a coward, she told herself sternly, but her heart was somewhere around her feet as she pushed open her door.

'Well, well. . .' Lloyd was seated on her settee, Lisa on one side of him and Wacky on the other. 'I wondered if you intended returning.'

'It's my apartment,' Sally said breathlessly.

'Oh, yes.' His dark eyes were watchful, carefully expressionless. 'And you're babysitting. Do you always leave your charges to fend for themselves?'

'They were out in the garden,' Sally told him, only the quaver in her voice betraying her nervousness. 'I've been watching them.'

'Oh, yes. The conscientious Dr Atchinson.'

'If you're going to be insulting then I think you should leave.'

He rose then, taking his walking-stick from the side of the settee where it had rested. He stood, tall and grim, his wide, mobile mouth set in a hard line.

'I agree I should leave,' he said smoothly. 'But before I go, I should say that I don't appreciate your meddling in my affairs.'

'Your affairs?' Somehow Sally made her eyes wide and innocent. 'I don't know what you mean, Dr Neale.'

'I think you do.'

She managed to smile at him and shook her head.

'Lisa. . .' Lloyd turned suddenly to the child on the settee. 'Lisa, I was down in the children's ward earlier this morning, and I heard they were having Frog in the Pond for morning tea. Sister said you'd be welcome to have some if you went now.'

'Frog in the Pond?' The child looked from Sally to Lloyd and back again, clearly aware of tension but unsure how to respond. 'What's Frog in the Pond?'

Lloyd shook his head. 'Good grief. The education of children nowadays is sadly lacking. Frog in the Pond, young Lisa, is chocolate frogs lurking in green jelly. Interested?'

It seemed she was. With a whoop of joy, Lisa took off out of the door.

'And now, Dr Atchinson. . .'

'Y-yes?' Sally's eyes were still innocent, but it was a Herculean effort to make them so.

'An hour ago I was engaged to be married. I'd like to know how you managed to interfere so fast.'

'I didn't.'

'No? If you're trying to tell me that Randolph Small threatening to knock me out if I laid one hand on Margaret ever again was none of your doing. . .'

'Oh, no. . .' The innocence flew from Sally's eyes to be replaced by laughter. The thought of Randolph

Small threatening to hit anyone was too much for her. Big, genial and decidedly pudgy was Randolph. The worst he might do to an opponent was probably to sit on them. 'I didn't think the man had it in him.'

Lloyd looked at her in baffled anger. 'You know why, then?'

'I. . .I suppose so.'

'So, what story have you concocted? Have you told him that I beat her? For heaven's sake, Sally. . .'

'Didn't they tell you?'

'All Margaret would do was cry, and Randolph started rabbiting on about his great-grandfather and about what a wonderful doctor you are, and that he was really sorry for me, but one step closer to Margaret and I'd be the one who was sorry. He said they'd been "torn asunder", for heaven's sake. . .'

'They're star-crossed lovers.'

'I beg your pardon?' Lloyd's face went blank with incredulity.

Somehow, Sally told him the story, and when she had finished Lloyd's anger hadn't abated one whit.

'I don't believe it,' he said harshly. 'Of all the stupid. . .'

'You don't?' Sally bit her lip and looked uncertainly up at him. 'I suppose. . .? I suppose you can't see the humour in this?'

'Humour!' Lloyd's anger exploded. 'How do you think this is supposed to make me feel?'

'Jilted?' Sally asked hopelessly. 'I'd never imagined Margaret as a wanton woman, oscillating between two lovers. How on earth could she have put aside her passion for Randolph to accept your very obliging offer?'

It was too much. She succumbed again to laughter.

'Sally Atchinson. . .' Lloyd's mouth twitched at the corners, and for a split second Sally saw the reflection of her laughter in his grey eyes. 'Do you know how close you're coming to having your ears boxed?'

'Wacky!' Sally tried to stifle her choking laughter. She called the dog over, put him purposely in front of her and managed to look Lloyd straight in the eye.

'You heard him, Wacky. He threatened me. Bite him on the leg.'

Wacky looked adoringly from one to the other and gave a hopeful woof.

'Sally. . .'

'I'm sorry, Lloyd,' Sally said placatingly. 'And if I thought you really loved her I'd be even more sympathetic. But she doesn't like your Beatles records. . .'

'If you think this is going to make one whit of difference to how I feel about you. . .'

The laughter died instantly from Sally's face. It was like a douche of ice-water.

'What. . .what do you mean?'

His anger faded slightly as the colour drained from Sally's face. Lloyd put up a hand as if to touch her. Then, recovering, the hand fell back to his side.

'Because I kissed you, Sally, you can't assume I mean anything more by it,' he said coldly. 'It didn't mean you had to try and destroy my relationship with Margaret.'

Silence.

'Is that why you think I referred them to genetic counselling?' Sally asked slowly—painfully. 'To free you to fall into my arms?'

'The thought just did cross my mind.' Lloyd's words and expression were sardonic. 'One moment you tell me you love me—the next you interfere in my relationship with my fiancée. . .'

'Of all the. . .' Anger welled up behind Sally's words. She could hardly speak. Wacky looked up at her and she put a hand on his head—to touch something solid.

'Margaret told me that she and Randolph couldn't

marry because of a genetic condition,' she said slowly. 'I'm a doctor, and I know what the facts are behind genetic disorders. What sort of doctor would I be if I hadn't told them the truth?'

'She didn't come to you for a medical consultation.'

'No. She came, like a good little chastened fiancée, on your instructions, to say she was sorry for being rude to me. She came because she wanted to please you. Only now. . . Hard as it may seem, Dr Neale, it seems she's not in love with you after all. She's in love with Randolph. And if you knew all along why she agreed to marry you—and didn't tell her. . .'

'I didn't know. For heaven's sake, Sally, if I'd known. . .'

'You might not have been tempted to accept such a paragon of a fiancée.'

'No. Yes. . .' Lloyd took a deep breath and his hand clenched white on his stick. 'So you didn't refer Margaret to the counsellor to get her out of the way. . .'

Again, silence. Wacky stirred uneasily at their feet. Clearly he felt the anger but didn't understand. He put his muzzle into Sally's hand and licked, seeking to impart comfort.

There was no comfort to give. Sally had never felt so exposed in her life—or so cold.

'Get out of my apartment, Lloyd Neale,' she whispered. 'Of all the arrogant. . .'

'If I'm arrogant, you're malicious.'

'For making two lovers happy?'

'You can't tell me you acted without malicious motive. I don't believe it.'

'You can believe anything you like,' Sally whispered. 'I don't care. But if you think I'm the least bit interested in you, Lloyd Neale. . . I might have fallen in love with you, but I'm not a complete fool—not yet, anyway. Margaret Howard's far better off with her

Randolph than with someone like you. So you can take your sour, sensible attitude to life and you can throw it wherever you intended throwing your Beatles records when you married Margaret. Because I'm not interested in you, or your life. Not now. Not ever. I wouldn't marry you if you were the last person on this earth. So get out of my apartment! Get out!'

They stood, glaring at each other, anger emanating in waves. It was a tangible presence in the room.

'Sally?' It was an uncertain voice from the door and Sally forced herself to look around.

'Sally, there's Frog in the Pond left over. Sister said I can bring some back for you if I want to. And. . .' The child looked worriedly at Lloyd. 'And Lloyd. . .'

'I'll go and get my own,' Lloyd said grimly.

'Will you get some for Sally too?'

'I don't think so,' Lloyd said slowly. 'I think Dr Atchinson can look after herself.'

Two cups of coffee later, Sally was still shaking. She sat and tried to read the morning paper, and then wandered around the apartment while Lisa and Wacky watched her with concerned eyes.

'We'll go for a walk,' Sally said finally. 'I'll just go and get out of my work clothes.'

'Great.' Lisa obviously approved of action. She didn't understand what was making Sally unhappy. The child picked up the newspaper Sally had abandoned and sat down with Wacky. 'I'll just read the comics to Wacky while I wait.'

It took Sally fifteen minutes to change. Actually, it took two minutes to slip on shorts, a soft blouse and sandals, but she took the opportunity to stare out of the window and reflect on the futility of errant hearts and traitorous men and life in general before returning to the living-room.

Lisa was no longer sitting comfortably on the settee

with Wacky. She was standing, the newspaper spread out before her on the kitchen bench, her face white as a sheet.

'They're cutting down Mum's trees,' she said blankly.

'What. . .?' One look at Lisa made Sally put her own misery aside. She stared down at the page Lisa was reading. It was a photograph of protesters being evicted from a logging camp. The caption read, 'Mount Willcanwe Giants to be Felled'.

'Mum's trees?' Sally queried, and the child burst into tears.

'My mum. My real mum, I mean—not Gina. She died when I was five. She had cancer. And the week before she died she took me up to Willcanwe and she made me sit under the big trees there. They're hundreds of feet high. And she said. . . She said that life kept on going. That those trees had been growing for five hundred years and maybe they'd be there in another five hundred. She said. . . She said there were permanent, important things that I could always use as a link to her and I had to remember that. I didn't know she was going to die when she said it but—but the trees. . . She said they were something that she loved and that I can love and my kids and my kids' kids can love. And, because we all love them, we're joined in some way still—even though my mum died. . .'

She choked on a sob and stopped. Her face crumpled and she buried her head in Sally's blouse.

Oh, help. . .

Sally cradled Lisa's head to her while she read the article. This was too much for her. She couldn't cope with Lisa's emotion as well as her own.

Struan would be back tonight. She could hand this one to Struan.

'Let's show this to your dad,' she said slowly, hating

herself for handing it over, yet not knowing what on earth to do. 'Maybe he knows someone who can help. And look—it says they're not due to be logged until the end of the month.'

'The end of the month. . .' Lisa pulled away and looked down at the paper. Clearly the end of the month seemed a lifetime away for a ten-year-old. 'That's. . . that's nearly a week.'

'Yes.'

The child sighed. 'Then. . . Then I guess there's something I can do by then.'

'I'm sure there is.' Sally produced a tissue and wiped the child's tearstained face. 'Now, let's go for this walk, shall we? I think we both need it.'

It was a long day and an even longer night.

Struan returned on the evening flight and reclaimed his daughter, his relief at the outcome of Pumpkin's operation tempered by his concern at Sally's decision to leave.

'Gina and I talked about it while Pumpkin was having her operation,' he told her. 'And we've had an idea.'

'I have to leave,' Sally said dully.

'Look, we know you and Lloyd don't get on. That's been obvious from the start. The problem's been compounded, though, because Lloyd's been acting anaesthetist and you haven't been able to get away from him. So. . . So, this morning, I rang around all the locum services and I've found us an anaesthetist.'

'An anaesthetist?'

'That's right,' Struan said patiently. 'A real live, qualified anaesthetist, who's willing to act as a locum here until our own anaesthetist returns. I've talked to Lloyd about it and he's agreed. It will mean you won't have to be in Lloyd's pocket all the time. And he can be here on Monday.'

'What's wrong with him?' Sally asked suspiciously, and Struan laughed. Any anaesthetist who was out of work and desperate enough to start a new job with two days' notice had to be under suspicion.

'He's an arrogant little toad,' Struan confessed. 'I met him for lunch and thought you might be better off sticking to Lloyd. But his professional credentials are impeccable and it's only for two months. And, if it means you can avoid Lloyd. . . Sally, we'd really like you to give this a go.'

'He can hardly be more arrogant than Lloyd,' Sally said slowly, and Struan shook his head.

'You really have brought out the worst in our Lloyd. It's a damned shame. Will you give this a go, please, Sally?'

Sally looked helplessly across at him. She so wanted to stay. It was like a physical ache. Maybe. . . Just maybe it could work.

'Yes, please,' she whispered. 'Thank you. . . Thank you, Struan.'

'You may well have saved our baby daughter's life.' Struan smiled. 'Half my kingdom is the usual fee, I've heard. This will have to do.' He picked up his sleepy Lisa. 'Now, let's get my first-born daughter home. Thank you for caring for her, Sally.'

'It was my pleasure.' Sally gave Lisa a swift hug. 'You tell your dad about the trees now, Lisa.'

'I will,' the child answered sleepily. 'Goodnight, Sally.'

Goodnight. . .

No way. Sally tossed in her lonely bed and agonised over her decision. Should she go? Or should she stay?

Who knew? Not Sally, that was for sure.

Midnight saw her staring sleeplessly at the moonlit ceiling. Finally she swore, rose, and slipped on her shorts and sandals. It was a balmy, star-lit night. The

surf was a gentle rush of water on the beach below.
It was a lovely night for a walk and a miserable night
to lie in bed and sweat about her bleak future.

She let herself quietly out of the apartment and
walked swiftly down to the beach.

She walked solidly for an hour, out of the cove and
along the vast expanse of beach stretching to the moonlit horizon. There was no sound but the gentle rush of
surf. Soon she abandoned her sandals and let the water
rush in over her toes, cooling her body and taking
some of the trouble from her tired mind.

What should she do? How could she stay here and
ignore Lloyd Neale? What was her body doing to her
to make her feel this way?

'I'm behaving like a fool,' she said into the rushing
waves. 'A love-sick teenager, throwing my heart at a
man who doesn't want it.'

She was so hot! Her toes felt lovely in the surf, but
trouble and fretting were making her tired body still
feel overheated. She wanted a swim. Slowly she
returned to the sheltered cove and stood staring out
at the black water. The moon cast a silver ribbon over
its surface but underneath was mysterious and black.

It was dangerous to swim at night.

'So who cares?' she said miserably to the moon.
'Who gives a damn about me, anyway?' She stared
resolutely out towards the entrance of the cove. She
could swim out to the ledge. Her hands crept to the
buttons of her blouse and she started undoing them.

'You'd be a fool, Sally Atchinson.'

Sally jumped about a foot. She swung around to find
Lloyd Neale limping down from the sand dunes, fifteen
feet from where she stood.

'What. . .? What are you doing here?' Her voice
was a croaking whisper.

'Trying to stop a hysterical woman throwing herself
into the ocean, by the look of it.' He kept coming until

he stood two feet away from her. 'Would you mind telling me what the hell you're doing?'

'I'm going for a swim.'

'Oh, yes,' he jeered. 'With the sting-rays and the sharks and all the other night-feeders.'

'It's none of your business what I do.'

'Granted. But I can't stand by and watch as you throw your life away. Much as I'd like to.'

Sally stared up at him. There was venom in his voice. This man hated her. Dear God, she loved him so much and he hated her. . .

To her horror she felt tears welling up in her eyes. She turned away, wiping her face furiously with her fingers.

'I'm not suiciding,' she whispered. 'Don't be stupid.'

'It's not me who's stupid.'

'No.' Sally caught her breath on a sob. 'I don't suppose it is. It's me again. Sally Atchinson. Stupid. Frivolous. Emotional. In short, everything you most despise. But you're never going to find your perfect mate, Lloyd Neale. In the end even your sensible Margaret was too emotional for you.'

'Margaret's emotions have nothing to do with you.'

'No.' She was sobbing now, hot tears spilling through her fingers as she fought for control. She didn't achieve it. 'Nothing's my business. Nothing in Gundowring. And nothing to do with you, Lloyd Neale. You can face your bleak, emotionless future by yourself. You can save every penny for a secure, barren life with no laughter and no love. And you can keep yourself safe for a ripe old age filled with nothing. Nothing! Because you won't risk anything any more, and if you don't risk then you don't win. You don't lose either, I guess. Not for you to throw your heart at someone who doesn't give a damn.'

'No.'

His single word stopped her, mid-tirade. He stood

motionless as Sally fought her rising helplessness. She tried to do up her blouse buttons but her fingers wouldn't work.

'Let me help. . .'

He put his hands on her shoulders and spun her round, but she pulled back as if burnt.

'Don't touch me, Lloyd. I can't bear it.'

'Sally, this is stupid. . .'

'It is, isn't it?' she said rigidly. 'That I should be making such a damned fool of myself. . .'

'It is foolish.'

'To feel like I feel?'

'To give in to that feeling.' His eyes were watchful in the moon's gentle rays. 'You can learn not to.'

'But why?' Sally choked on a sob. 'I think. . .I think I'd rather be dead than learn not to love.'

Silence. Then, before she knew what he intended, Lloyd leaned forward and took her hand.

'Do you want a swim?' he asked gently.

'No. Yes. . .' The gentleness of his voice went through her like a knife. 'Don't touch me. . .'

'Come on, then,' he told her, ignoring her tugging to be released. 'You're never going to sleep while you're this emotional. Around the other side of the cove is a rock pool. At this tide level it's overflowing— a wonderful place to swim, free from marauding nasties.'

'Marauding nasties. . .' Sally choked on a hysterical sob. 'Does that mean you?'

'I'll be lifesaver,' he promised. 'I'll hardly watch at all, much less maraud.'

He brooked no protest. Leaving his stick where it lay on the sand, Lloyd led her towards the rocks at the edge of the cove.

'Your leg's getting stronger,' Sally whispered.

'I've been taking my surgeon's advice.' To her fury she heard laughter in his voice, and she wrenched her hand—but she wasn't to be released.

'You need a swim, Dr Atchinson. Twenty laps of solid physical work to make you sleep tonight.'

He was right. It was what she needed. But hardly with Lloyd Neale watching her.

The rock pool was magnificent. Sally had been here during the day but hadn't realised its potential. At low tide it was a rock-ledge between the cove and the sea, with a series of deep pools behind it. Now it was one long stretch of deep water, fresh surf spilling over the wall as each wave rolled in. It was safe and it was just what she needed.

But not with Lloyd.

'You don't need to lifesave,' she muttered.

'I'd be negligent if I didn't,' he said lightly. 'And one thing I'm not, Dr Atchinson, is negligent.'

'Well, hooray for you.' She turned to the water and dived straight in.

It felt wonderful. The water caressed her troubled body as nothing else could, cooling and comforting. Left to herself she would have drifted, floating on the buoyant salt surface. But now. . .

Now Lloyd was watching her, and she was too self-conscious. She turned her head towards the other end of the long pool, and started swimming.

Ten long, slow laps later she had almost forgotten that Lloyd was watching her. Almost, but not quite. He was a dark, brooding presence at the end of the pool, his crouched figure silhouetted against the moon.

Watching. . .

Fifteen laps. . . Tiredness was beginning to take its toll. Soon she would have to emerge to face him.

He was like a statue—immobile. His dark shape gave nothing away, and yet. . .

And yet if Sally could have made him somehow disappear she wouldn't have. Just his presence warmed her.

Crazy. . .

She reached the end of the pool where Lloyd sat waiting, clung to the rock at the edge and pulled herself up. Lloyd's hands came down, grasped her wrists and lifted her on to the ledge.

'I suppose you didn't bring a towel,' he said, and sighed as she shook her head. 'And you had to swim in your clothes.'

What clothes? Sally looked ruefully down at herself in the moonlight. She hadn't put on a bra and her wispy blouse had faded to a damp film. It clung to her wet body, revealing all. She put her hands to her breasts self-consciously.

'Take my shirt.' He was hauling the shirt from his back. 'Take your wet one off and have mine.'

'No. I don't want——'

'Take it off, Sally, or I'll rip the thing off you. Struan and I aren't paying for a locum anaesthetist only to have our surgeon succumb to pneumonia.'

No. Of course not. How sensible.

She had managed to refasten only two of her blouse buttons before her swim but it took her unsteady fingers moments to undo those. Then, before she could turn away from Lloyd, his hands came out and he lifted her wet blouse from her body.

It fell to his feet. In his hands he held his dry shirt. He stood, bare-chested in the moonlight, holding his shirt out to her, and Sally looked up at him and any words she could think of died unsaid.

The shirt was between them—in his hands. She didn't take it. She couldn't, and finally, finally Lloyd's hands fell. The shirt dropped to lie on top of Sally's.

'Sally. . .' It was a throaty whisper—the sound of a man whose iron will was breaking. 'Sally. . .'

And then, somehow, she was in his arms, and his chest was hard against her breasts. Skin against skin—

her wetness against the hard, male muscular body that she loved. . .

She gave a sob of confusion, but it was washed away in the sound of the surf.

They stood, locked together, motionless, for long minutes. Sally could feel his heart hammer within his chest and she knew the fight that was warring within. She should pull away. She should. . .

She could no more do so than fly. She was where she was meant to be. Her heartbeats matched his. She felt them synchronise, melding into the one sensation. One heartbeat. . .

He felt it. She could feel the rigidity slowly leave his body. The battle had been fought and lost—or fought and won.

'Dear heaven. . .' His mouth was in her hair. 'It's not fair that you're so beautiful. You've bewitched me, woman. You know that? Bewitching, enchanting surgeon. . .'

She raised her face then. For a long, long moment they stood, eyes locked in the moonlight, and then slowly, as if he was approaching something infinitely precious, he bent his head to kiss her.

Dear God. . .

She had died and gone to heaven. This was how she had always imagined his lips could feel. This was the kiss of a man surrendering to his woman. Tender and yet possessive. Sweet and salt. . . The feeling was indescribable. Shards of joy were threading through her body and she heard herself moan in exquisite pleasure.

His tongue was demanding. Her lips parted, enabling him to explore the sweet recesses of her mouth. Her own tongue met his, possessing him, wanting to feel every part of him.

She felt naked against him. She was wearing only her flimsy shorts and they were as nothing. She could feel her breasts quiver, erect against the hardness of his chest. Lloyd felt them too. His hands came around to cradle each in turn and then his lips dropped to kiss gently.

'Dear God,' he whispered into the darkness. 'God help me, Sally, I want you.'

Sally ran her fingers through his thatch of fair hair. 'You don't have to want me,' she whispered simply. 'You only want something you don't have—and you have me. I've always been yours. Now and forever. I've told you that.'

He broke away then, backing to stand at arms' length.

'Just like that?' he said. 'No pride? No reservations?'

'How can there be pride when there's love?' she whispered tremulously. 'And I love you. I think I always have—I just hadn't met you until these last few weeks. I always knew that you'd be somewhere . . . waiting. . .'

He gave a sharp exclamation and gathered her to him. His hands pulled her waist hard to him, holding her possessively.

'How can you be so sure?'

'I'm not sure of you,' she murmured, putting her finger up to trace the lines of pain etched on his face. 'I'm only sure of how I feel.'

'But what if I can't give love? What if I'm not capable?'

'I don't know if I have enough love for both of us,' she said simply. 'But I'll try.'

'Sally. . .'

'Mmm.' Her face was nestled on his chest and his lips were in her hair. She felt on fire.

'I think. . .I think we'd better go back to my apartment.'

'Why?' She knew why, but she desperately, desperately wanted to hear him say it.

'Because I'm moving past the point of no return,

my Sally,' he whispered. 'And if you're not intending to stop me. . .'

'I couldn't if I wanted to.'

'Then we'd better take precautions,' he murmured. 'Because, while you're taking a chance on love, I don't think we should take a chance on anything else.'

'Very sensible,' she murmured, her lips threading through the hairs on his chest.

'That's me,' Lloyd said huskily. 'Very sensible. I don't think!'

CHAPTER TEN

SALLY woke to joy.

It was all around her, sweeping through her as consciousness returned with such force that she almost cried out with it.

She didn't. Encircled in Lloyd's arms she turned to her love and watched the pain eased from his face with sleep.

Dear God, she loved him so. Last night, for the first time, she had been able to ease those lines of past pain from his tired face. She had been able to make him smile, and laugh, and forget for a tiny while that the weight of the world was on his shoulders.

If only it could be forever.

Maybe it could. Maybe. . . The tiny flame of hope that had kindled as he kissed her last night had grown and grown. Now it was almost overwhelming in its intensity. If only he could learn to trust the world again. If only he could accept her love. . .

He stirred then, his arm tightening around her naked waist as sleep faded.

'Mmm. You feel nice, my Sally. Warm. . .'

'Better than a hot-water bottle?' she whispered, and felt a chuckle deep within his chest. She exulted at the sensation. To make Lloyd laugh again. . .

He turned to nuzzle her hair. 'Carrots,' he teased. 'Did they call you that at school?'

'All the time,' she confessed. 'And freckle-face.'

'I like 'em.' He stirred, lifting his body so that he was looking down at her face. 'Did you know you have a freckle right at the end of your nose, Sally Atchinson?'

'No. . . I. . .'

'And that it's demanding to be kissed—right this minute?'

'Well,' Sally whispered breathlessly, 'what are you going to do about it?'

'I'm going to oblige, of course. And I always play fair. What I do to one I have to do to the others. What a fortunate thing you seem to have such a lot of freckles, my Sally.'

Afterwards they lay, limp and happy, linked by entwined arms.

'Sally. . .' Lloyd's voice seemed to come from far away.

'Mmm?'

'You didn't tell me you were a virgin.'

'You didn't ask.'

'Neither I did.' He stirred then, moving away from her in the bed. He sat up and looked out of the window at the sea beyond. 'Sally, what you're offering. . .'

'What I'm giving.'

He shook his head. 'God knows, I've done enough damage already,' he said unsteadily. 'I'm not going to lie to you. Sally, what I'm feeling for you. . . Well, you're right. It's something that. . . Well, I've never felt like this before. But whether it's the basis for marriage. . .'

'I'm not asking for marriage,' Sally whispered unsteadily. 'It's you who wants the brick veneer and the retirement package.'

'So. . .' He didn't turn. He didn't look at her. 'So I use you for as long as I want and then I let you go?'

You'll never let me go, Sally said under her breath. Please. . . She didn't say anything, though. She moved across to his side of the bed and ran her finger down the scar at the base of his spine.

'Does this still ache?'

'Sometimes. Sally. . .'

She put her lips on the white line of the scar and ran a stream of kisses down the old wound. Her fingers came up to knead his spine gently.

'I can heal you again,' she whispered. 'All you have to do is give me a chance.'

'Sally. . .'

'Lie down,' she ordered. 'On your front. I'm going to give you a massage that no physiotherapist has ever heard of.'

'Healing surgeon. . .'

'Shut up and lie down,' she ordered, and he turned to her and smiled.

'Bossy. . .'

'You'll get used to it.'

'Yes, Doctor,' he said meekly, and submitted to the pleasures of her hands.

In the days to come Sally would remember that Sunday with disbelief. They'd slept until nearly noon, smuggled Sally around to her apartment to shower and dress and had done their respective ward-rounds. No medical emergencies had marred their day. They had taken a picnic on to the beach, walking for as far as Lloyd's leg would take him until they knew they were unobserved by any mortal soul except each other. Then they'd eaten and swum and made love and talked and slept. . . And made love again. And again.

Let it go on forever, Sally had thought dreamily as they walked back along the beach after dark. Lloyd's hand had been round her waist. They had been walking on firm sand, his stick making a third footprint.

'It's a signature.' Sally smiled. 'Everyone will know we've been here.'

'The tide will wash away all evidence,' Lloyd told her, and for some reason the thought made Sally's heart shrivel. A cold wave of foresight washed over her, as though she knew it had to end.

That night they made love as though tomorrow the world would end. They clung together even in sleep.

'It will end,' Lloyd said softly as he prepared to leave her at dawn. He touched her face with his hand. 'There's no such thing as perfection, my Sally.'

'There is,' she said obstinately, clinging to his hand. 'We have it.'

He shook his head. 'It's always flawed. I hope to heaven I'm wrong, but. . .' He sighed. 'I remember the feeling after I qualified as a doctor. I was on top of the world. I had a girlfriend too. Beautiful. . . Or at least I thought so. She stayed in Melbourne when I came to Gundowring, but she was going to join me. Then. . . Well, the world came crashing down. I broke my back and Jane didn't want to know about it. For a while they thought I might be a paraplegic—and Jane just ran.

'Then, when I finally got back on my feet. . . Well, things started to go OK. I trusted again, I guess. I started to enjoy being a doctor and to enjoy my income. I spent a bit on some silly things—great holidays, things like that. And then my brother mortgaged my parents' home and his business went bust. I didn't have the money to bail him out—so my parents lost their home and my brother suicided. So. . .'

'So you're darned if you'll expose yourself again.'

He turned to her then, and kissed her lightly on the nose. 'I think. . .I think what I'm trying to say, my Sally, is that I'm starting to feel very exposed right now. And it's scaring me to death.'

He'd learn, Sally thought now. Given time, he'd learn to trust.

Sally did her Monday ward-round with a light heart and she had comments all round.

'April and May,' Henry hooted as she changed his dressings. 'And June and July thrown in for good measure, I reckon. You know you have roses in your cheeks this morning?' he demanded, and Sally blushed.

'Ho, hoo. . .' He chuckled with delight. Then he frowned. 'Only thing I can't figure. . . Margaret Howard came in early this morning with medical claim forms—and she looks the same. Blooming! Doc Neale's not two-timing the both of you, is he?'

'Tell me, Henry,' Sally whispered conspiratorially. 'What ring was Margaret Howard wearing this morning?' She had seen Margaret an hour before. Margaret had given her a sheepish grin and had held up her hand for inspection.

'Can't say I noticed——' He stopped and frowned. 'Yes, I did. A ruddy great cluster of diamonds. Not the sort of ring Doc Neale would——' He stopped again, obviously thinking back to the hand that had filled in the medical forms the week before. 'She wasn't wearing that ring last week.'

Sally grinned happily down at him. 'There you go, then, Sherlock Holmes. See if you can solve the mystery by lunchtime.' She put the final sticking plaster on the dressing. 'In fact, you'd better solve it by lunchtime because I'm going to send you home this afternoon. If you want to go. . .'

'Do I want to?' His smile lit his scarred face from ear to ear. 'You're a doc in a million, Doc Atchinson.'

By lunchtime the hospital was buzzing with gossip. Everyone seemed to have their own version of the weekend's events. Margaret Howard had removed Lloyd's photograph from her desk and Randolph Small had telephoned her three times already. Contrary to looking a jilted man, however, Lloyd looked relaxed and, well. . .

'Happy,' Matron told Sally confidentially as she helped Sally examine Lorna Dalziel. 'I haven't seen that look of strain leave his face for a very long time.

If it's any of your doing, my dear. . .'

Sally just shook her head and smiled, but Matron saw the colour in her cheeks and drew her own conclusions.

Sally's happiness lasted a mere two more hours.

She'd been consulting, seeing one surgical case after the other. As she farewelled her last patient, promising to meet him the next morning on the operating table, Lloyd knocked on the door. He smiled as she stood up and came around the desk.

'Tired, my Sally?' He touched her lightly on the hair and she closed her eyes in pleasure.

'Yes,' she whispered.

'If it's any consolation,' he teased, 'you deserve to be. Come and meet my replacement anaesthetist.'

'We hardly need him now,' Sally said doubtfully. 'Now we've agreed to bury the hatchet.'

'We do, you know,' he told her. 'I never intended acting as anaesthetist for a full-time surgeon. My medical practice is suffering—and I've other things to occupy my thoughts now.'

'Oh, yes?' she asked cheekily. 'Like what?'

'Like you.' He hugged her hard against him and they walked out into the reception area with Sally's face burnt crimson. There was soon going to be little left for the hospital staff to guess, Sally thought.

'I've left Peter in the tea-room,' he told her. Lloyd led Sally along the corridor, opened the door and Sally stopped dead.

Her bubble of joy faded and the nightmate flooded back.

Peter Grimble. . . A pedantic little man, unpopular with staff and patients alike at the hospital where Sally had last worked, Peter had been asked to leave three months ago, and no one had cared much where he went.

Peter. . .

He looked up from his mug of coffee and his smooth smile of greeting faded from his face.

'You,' he whispered.

'P-Peter.' Sally bit her lip. She should have asked. Never in a million years had she imagined that Peter Grimble would come here.

Still, Peter was a competent anaesthetist. It was only his appalling rudeness that got him into trouble.

'So this is where you bolted.' He smiled silkily. 'A nice little country job, far from the scales of justice.'

'Peter, for heaven's sake. . .' Sally's face drained of colour. Surely he wouldn't bring it up? Not even Peter could be that vindictive.

It seemed he could. Peter had been out of work for three months, seething with injustice, and the sight of Sally in a secure job was enough to bring out his worst. He glanced up at Lloyd. 'I don't know about acting as anaesthetist for Dr Atchinson,' he told him. 'I'm not one for abetting murderers.'

'Peter!' Sally's fingers dug into her palms. 'That's. . . That's not fair, and you know it. There was a full investigation and I was cleared at the inquest.'

'A clever murderer,' he agreed. He smiled. 'Heck, Sally, I'm not saying I blame you. Maybe I'd have done the same in your place. I just know I wouldn't like to be under your knife when you're angry—and maybe I'm not going to stick around and act as anaesthetist while you operate under those conditions.'

'What on earth are you talking about?' Lloyd's eyes had been moving from one to another. His instinctive dislike of this man was deepening—Sally could see it in his face—but he wanted to know, for all that.

'Peter's talking about an operation I performed four months ago,' Sally said dully. 'On a young car accident victim. His injuries were similar to Gary's—the boy in the car accident up on Mount Mendy. And, like Gary, he died.'

'Did it again, did you sweetheart?' Peter said pleasantly. 'Getting good at it, are we?'

'Peter, shut up,' Sally said desperately. 'You know I tried. You know I didn't want him to die. I worked so hard to save him. . .'

'That's not what the police thought, though, is it?' Peter smiled. 'They even had three different surgeons at the post-mortem. And one of them said he shouldn't have died. It was only your boss and his paid lackey who saved your bacon—with their "unpredictable death after such severe trauma". He bled to death, though, didn't he sweetheart? And you could have stopped it.'

'I couldn't . . I didn't. . .' The nightmare was all around her, flooding back from the dark recesses of her mind where she'd locked it at the end of the interminable inquest.

'Why on earth would Sally have wanted to kill him?' Lloyd sounded bemused rather than concerned. He stared down at Peter, his dislike intensifying in his gaze.

'Oh, she had the strongest motive.' Peter was clearly enjoying himself. He would have liked a larger audience, but this one would do—and Sally Atchinson seemed to be suffering nicely.

'The boy was drunk,' Peter continued, relishing each word. 'He was driving a car full of kids. He pulled out to pass another car and slammed straight into the car coming the other way. Unfortunately, the driver of the oncoming car was Sally's father.'

Lloyd turned to stare at Sally. Her white face confirmed Peter's words.

'And. . .?' he said slowly.

'Well, you can imagine the scene,' Peter continued. 'You'll have seen Casualty after a multi-car pile-up. The car the kid passed slammed into the other two so we ended up with nine people in Casualty, four of them dead and the other five in dire straits. They brought the living in first, of course. Sally was prepping the driver—getting him ready for Theatre—when a couple of policemen came to tell her what the kid had done to her father.'

'Sally's father was dead?'

'Dead as a doornail,' Peter said in satisfaction. 'And our Dr Atchinson looked down at the kid she was supposed to be operating on and said she wouldn't operate.'

'C-couldn't,' Sally whispered. There was a difference.

'Neither she should have,' Lloyd said harshly. 'Someone else should have taken over.'

'Not as easy as it sounds, old man,' Peter said. 'Two in the morning. All theatres on the go. Sally had tried to stabilise before operating and the kid was drunk. She was the last surgeon to take her case to Theatre and all the other surgeons were occupied—including our two call-back surgeons. There was only Sally.' He smiled. 'I remember the way she looked down at the kid on the trolley. Her face. . . She said. . . She said, "I'll kill him if I do."'

Peter smiled again. 'So she operated and she did kill him. All very satisfactory, as far as I can see, but maybe a trifle lacking in the rudiments of justice.'

Lloyd frowned down at Peter and then his face turned to Sally. 'What the heck. . .? Did you make that threat?'

'Yes. . . No.' Sally bit her lip so hard that it bled. It had been so difficult to make them see. It was still impossible.

'My father. . .' she whispered. 'He meant so much to me. . .'

'That you'd kill for him?'

'No!' Her eyes flew up to Lloyd's, and to her amazement she saw doubt in his eyes. Doubt. . .

'My hands. . .' she whispered. 'My hands were shaking. I was feeling sick. I was frightened that I couldn't do it. He needed someone competent. Yes. . . I was scared I'd kill him. . . Because of my hands. . .'

'But you operated anyway?'

'There wasn't anyone else. The anaesthetic. . . Peter had already had him prepped. We had to go. . .'

'And your hands stopped shaking,' Peter said in satisfaction. 'You took a deep breath and you operated, with cold, clean precision. And he died.'

'I don't have to listen to this.' Sally looked pleadingly up at Lloyd. 'Do you think I could possibly have. . .?'

The doubt was still in his eyes.

She closed hers. The nightmare slammed back through her, worse than ever before. At least her boss and her family had believed her. But to have Lloyd look at her like that. . .

How could she have ever dreamed that he would love her? He couldn't know her. Not if for one moment he could think. . .

There was no possible defence against that look. If he could possibly think that she would kill there was nothing there to build on.

'I was leaving Gundowring on Friday,' she said bleakly. 'I'll buy my plane ticket this morning.'

She walked out and closed the door behind her.

Lloyd caught up with her five minutes later. Sally was back in her apartment, staring bleakly out of the window at the sea.

How could she have dreamed that it was over? A nightmare like that, filtering through the rest of her life. . .

Again and again she went through the procedures she had used that night. She had been so frightened. She had stared down at the boy's face on the table and she had felt anger—anger stronger than anything she had ever known. It had made her feel nauseous.

And then she had looked again, and the boy had whimpered in his drugged sleep. A stupid, drunk kid who had wiped out three of his friends and her beloved father with one careless action. If he lived, he was going to have to face the courts, as well as the months and months of excruciating rehabilitation.

She still shouldn't have operated. Her shock at her father's death was making her sick, but if she was the only one. . . If she was the only surgeon between this youth and death. . .

She had had no choice. So, yes, her face had set into rigid concentration. She had fought her shaking fingers, battling them into rigid submission. She had operated with absolute precision—with meticulous care.

And the boy had died under her hands.

He would have died anyway. That was what her boss had said. He had come on duty the next morning and shouted the place down when he realised what she had been asked to do. He had threatened to sack anyone who as much as whispered that Sally had been less than competent—but then the boy's family had discovered the relationship between the woman who had operated on their boy and the man the boy had killed.

They had wanted blood. Any blood. They had employed smart doctors and smart lawyers and gone straight for Sally with iron determination. Peter hadn't helped either. Despite his boss's threat, Peter had smirked and smarmed and insinuated during the inquest, until Sally had felt sure they would find against her.

They couldn't, though. The boy's injuries had truly been dreadful. There was no way any doctor could have stood in court and said absolutely that if Sally hadn't operated then the boy would have lived.

So she had been exonerated, and only her hospital

had been criticised for letting her operate. There was criticism of Sally's operating even in that, though.

Those ghastly few days flooded through and through Sally's mind as she stared out of the window and looked her future bleakly in the face.

Lloyd didn't knock.

He came in silently, limped to where she stood and put his hand on her shoulder. She didn't turn.

'Sally. . .'

'What?' Her voice was devoid of all expression. She felt numb and sick.

'Do you want to tell me about it?'

'No.'

'Sally. . .' He sighed. 'I think you must.'

She turned then, and faced him. 'I didn't kill him, Lloyd,' she said dully. 'Is that what you want to know?'

'Tell me what happened.'

'No.' She shrugged his hands off her shoulders. 'I won't. Not while you look at me like that—you stand there judging. . .'

'I can't judge unless I know.'

'And you don't know me, so you can't judge.'

'Sally, for heaven's sake. . . This is so important. . .'

'Important?' Her face was cold. She put her hands to her cheeks, seeking warmth, and found none. 'It's not important, Lloyd. Not unless you think I could possibly have killed him. And then. . .'

'But why didn't you tell me?'

'Why should I? I operated and he died. It's happened before and it'll happen again. I'm a surgeon.'

'But to operate on the man who killed you father. . .'

'Stop it!' Sally turned away to the window again. She put her hands on the window-ledge, needing its solid support. When she spoke again she had her voice under control.

'Lloyd, you don't trust life. I accept that. It's dealt you some pretty heavy blows. But it's dealt me a few too, believe it or not, and I haven't judged and condemned the whole world because of it.'

'I haven't——'

'Judged me?' Sally shook her head. 'No. But you're wondering. And I don't want a love like that, Lloyd. I thought I could make a difference—but if every accuser is going to make you look like that. . . As if I'm wearing some sort of disguise, which some day will disappear to reveal the true me—a true self you always suspected. Frivolous, uncaring. . . Murdering. . .'

'For heaven's sake, Sally. . . You're being stupid. All you have to do is tell me.'

'That's just it,' Sally whispered. 'I shouldn't have to tell you. I want you. . . I want you to know.'

Silence.

'I guess I can't,' he said heavily. 'I trusted Jane—and then, as soon as I broke my back, she turned into someone I didn't know.'

'I'm not Jane.' Sally bit her lip. Her fingers clenched on the window-sill and she closed her eyes. 'Lloyd, I'm not part of your past. And I'm starting to think. . . I guess I know. . .that I'm not part of your future either.'

'Sally. . .'

'Go away,' she whispered. 'Please, Lloyd. . . Leave me alone.'

'If that's what you want. . .'

'That's what I want.'

CHAPTER ELEVEN

PETER GRIMBLE left on the evening plane. Heaven knew what Lloyd had told him to get rid of him, but Sally didn't care that he had gone.

If Gundowring didn't have a surgeon then it didn't need an anaesthetist.

Struan came to see her that evening. He looked tired and harassed, and Sally felt a pang of remorse at the trouble she had put him to.

'Lloyd told me what happened,' he said briefly. 'I'm appalled, Sally. Won't you reconsider?'

'I can't.' Sally spread her hands. 'Surely you can see that?'

'For heaven's sake, Sally, no one here thinks you could possibly have acted maliciously.'

'Lloyd does.'

'Then Lloyd's a fool.'

'Yes.' Sally closed her eyes on sudden tears and turned away. 'I'm sorry, Straun. Please. . . You and Gina have been good friends.'

'But you can't stay because of Lloyd?'

'I can't stay because of Lloyd,' she agreed dully, and by the way Struan nodded, and the swift hug he gave her as he left, she knew that he, at least, understood.

So she only had to get through four more days. Four days of the routine operations she had booked. Four days of seeing Lloyd, grim and silent at the other end of the operating table.

And then it would be finished.

Lloyd let her be. He didn't approach her, and Sally's prediction came true. Their only contact was in

167

Theatre, and their only communication was the terse, verbal requirements of their job.

Tuesday night. Wednesday. . .

Sally rang an agency in Melbourne and found a list of country practices requiring surgeons. She read them through with a heavy heart. Queensland, maybe— somewhere well away from Gundowring.

Australian Volunteers Abroad would get her further. They were asking for volunteers to go to Rwanda. Maybe there. . .

She couldn't make any decisions feeling the way she did. She'd take two weeks off and stay with her cousin—try to clear her head.

Try to empty her heart.

She still hadn't told Lisa she was leaving. On Wednesday night she went to bed with the resolve to tell the child the next morning.

At midnight, just as her first troubled dream began, the phone rang.

'Sally, is Lisa there?'

It was Struan. Gina was still in Melbourne with Pumpkin, but Struan had taken Lisa and Wacky home.

'No.' Sally frowned into the darkness. 'Why should she be here?'

'I told her tonight that you were leaving.' Struan sighed. 'She was upset, but I thought she went to sleep. I checked her an hour ago and she was fine. Ten minutes ago I checked her again, before I went to bed myself, and her window's open. Both she and Wacky are gone.'

Oh, no. . .

'She and Wacky,' Sally said slowly, thinking things through.

'Yes.' Struan sighed again. 'If Wacky wasn't gone then I'd be frantic, but no one's going to abduct a child *and* a dog the size of Wacky. Besides, if any stranger came near, Wacky would raise the roof. Lisa's dressed and gone—and it's my guess she's coming to the hospital to find you. But. . . It's only five minutes away by foot, and she could have left an hour ago. She should be there by now.'

'I'll go and check the apartment,' Sally promised. 'Maybe she's in the living-room—or out with Night Sister.'

'I'll drive slowly in to the hospital while you do,' Struan told her. 'Maybe she's still on the road. If she's not at the hospital by the time I arrive then I'm calling the police.'

He hung up, a worried man, and Sally flicked on the light.

'Lisa?' she called.

No answer.

Swearing softly to herself, Sally hauled on jeans, T-shirt and sandals and made her way out through the apartment. She checked the spare room and the living-room, and then, feeling silly, checked cupboards and under beds. No child.

She walked to the door of the apartment and stopped dead.

The trees.

Lisa's beloved trees. Sally had meant to make sure that Struan knew of Lisa's distress at the cutting down of her mother's trees but, caught up in her own emotional upheaval, she had forgotten all about it.

How could she?

'You stupid, stupid fool,' she told herself angrily, as she wrenched open her living-room door and hurried down the hospital corridor.

It was no use trying to telephone Struan. He'd be driving here slowly, checking every inch of the roadside as he went. If Lisa had disappeared without telling him then chances were she'd try not to be caught.

Should she ring the police straight away, then? Sally's feet broke into a run and she rounded the hospital corridor fast—to run straight into Lloyd.

This time she didn't knock him over. He wasn't using his stick, and he caught her with both hands and steadied her.

'You're never going to learn, are you, Dr Atchinson?' he snapped in fury.

'Lloyd, have you seen Lisa?'

Her fear broke through Lloyd's anger. He stood, staring down at her, and then slowly shook his head.

'Lorna Dalziel's drip just packed up.' Anger was replaced by swift concern. 'I've been in her ward for the past fifteen minutes. Is Lisa missing?'

'Struan's just phoned.' Briefly she outlined the problem. 'And Lloyd. . .I think Lisa may have gone to Mount Willcanwe.'

'Wilcanwe. . . That's four miles south of here. She'd never go there at night.'

'But she read last week that they're cutting down the trees there—and her mother loved them. She might go. . .'

'She wouldn't.' Lloyd's grip tightened on Sally's shoulders. 'For heaven's sake, Sally, use your head. The child's only ten. What on earth do you think she could do at midnight to stop the loggers cutting down the trees?'

'The loggers. . .' Sally's face lost any vestige of colour remaining. 'They posted someone to stop Gary and Melinda. . .'

'And I suppose you're suggesting they'll shoot Lisa?'

'No. . . Yes. . .' Sally broke away from him and stared up at his face. Her eyes were huge with horror. 'Lloyd, we have to go.'

His eyes widened in incredulity. 'You're not serious, Sally? Lisa will be on the road between here and the hospital. Struan will find her.'

'And if he doesn't?'

'Then we worry.' He sighed and shook his

head. 'Sally, you're letting your emotions sway your reason. You can't go haring up to Mount Willcanwe without good reason. Heaven knows, *you* will end up being shot. Go and make yourself a cup of coffee and wait.'

'Like a sensible little doctor,' Sally whispered. She stared up at him with something akin to hatred. 'So you won't come with me to Mount Willcanwe?' she whispered.

'There's no need.' He frowned at her. 'Stop being emotional for once, Sally. Think this through sensibly while you have your coffee. Lisa will arrive here any minute.'

Sally shook her head. 'I know Lisa,' she said softly. 'She's emotional too. Not like the sensible, stable, worthy Dr Neale.'

'Sally, you're being silly,'

Silly. . . The word hung between them. Silly.

'Maybe I am,' Sally said at last. 'But I'd rather go on a silly wild-goose chase up to Mount Willcanwe than sit here and drink coffee and run the risk of her being there alone. That's what love is all about, I guess. Taking the risk of being silly.' Her voice trailed off as she choked on a sob. 'So. . . So you can take your coffee, Dr Neale,' she managed to whisper, 'and you can dump it right where it hurts most. I'm going to the mountain.'

Thirty seconds later, Sally was behind the wheel of her car. It had taken her that long to decide what had to be done.

It would be best if she could find Struan, but Struan was somewhere to the north, searching roads. She could phone the police, but, like Lloyd, they might decide to wait.

And she'd waited long enough. Four miles. . . Not so far, especially if Lisa was frightened and walking fast. If Lisa was moving fast then she could be on the mountain in an hour, and it had been over an hour since Struan had seen her.

She could be there now.

And if the loggers had someone posted, guarding their trees. . .

'Dear God,' Sally whispered into the night, shoving her foot down hard on the accelerator. 'Please let Lloyd be right and me be wrong. Please let me be silly.'

The road to Mount Willcanwe swung sharply inland, just out of town. Sally drove swiftly, her eyes straining ahead into the darkness. The roadside here was heavily wooded, but at a guess. . .

'If I were ten and in a hurry I'd stick to the road,' Sally told herself. If Lisa was hiding behind trees on the roadside there was no way Sally could find her.

She had to reach the greatest danger. If she could get to Mount Willcanwe and make sure there were no loggers. . . Or at least let the loggers know that the person up there was a ten-year-old. . .

'Surely they wouldn't be so foolish, after what they did to Gary and Melinda?' she whispered. 'Surely. . .'

Then the car was climbing, up through the foothills at the base of the mount. The road here was narrow, with dense bush at either side. Finally, in front of the car, was a huge sign. 'Willcanwe Logging Site. Trespassers Prohibited'.

So where were these special trees? Sally stopped the car and climbed out, straining eyes and ears in the darkness.

'Lisa. . .' she yelled. 'Lisa. . . Wacky. . .'

Nothing.

'Can anyone hear me? There's a child lost up here. Can anyone hear me?'

Anyone waiting to shoot trespassers on sight would surely have heard that in the stillness. Sally looked up helplessly. The mountain loomed dark and forbidding in the night.

This area had already been logged. Sally could see that. There were tracks into the bush and debris at the roadside telling of recent logging.

Those giants. . . Those beloved trees. . .

They're more likely to be up at the top, she said to herself. If Lisa's mum went there—and loved them— they're more likely to be up high, where she could sit underneath them and see the sea. . .

Crazy logic, but she had nothing else to go on. Sally cast one more look at the 'Trespassers Prohibited' sign, shrugged, and restarted her car. She pointed its nose to the top.

Just before she reached the top she passed a truck. Sally slowed as her headlights glinted on dull metal. The battered tray-truck was pulled well off the road, half-hidden by bush.

Her heart sank. It had to be a logger's truck.

She parked the car beside the truck and left he headlights burning. She didn't want anyone to think she was creeping around in the dark.

'Is anyone here?' she yelled at the top of her lungs. Then, reverting to pure Australian bushcraft, she cupped her hands and tried the time-honoured, 'Coo-eee!'

Nothing.

The bitumen road petered out. A rough logging-track lay ahead, and Sally wasn't game to risk her little car on those deep furrows. She'd be stuck within yards.

So now what? Stay here? Wait?

It seemed crazy to go any further. She knew there was a logging-truck here, so chances were it was attached to someone. And she didn't know for sure that Lisa was here.

'Lisa!' she yelled helplessly in the dark, and her voice was met by an echo. It wasn't an echo of her voice, though. It was the report of a gun.

Dear God. . .

The sound came from above, on the ridge of the mountain. Sally stared into the night, trying to force vision into her night-blind eyes. Then, before she had time to think, she found herself stumbling along the track, screaming as she went.

'No. Stop. It's a child. Don't shoot. . .'

Another shot, and somewhere above she heard a scream. Lisa. . . It was Lisa.

She yelled back, and then something catapulted into her in the dark. Something wet and large and hairy. Sally stumbled backwards and lay flat on her back. Wacky was covering every inch of her that he could.

'Oh, Wacky. . . Good dog. . . Oh, Wacky. . .' And then the sickening realisation. If Wacky was here then so was Lisa, and it must definitely have been Lisa that she had heard scream.

'No. . .' Sally was screaming into the dark, on her feet again and stumbling forward, her hand tight on Wacky's collar. He seemed to realise what was required, hauling her forward as if guiding her to his mistress.

It was more important to make a noise.

'It's a child,' she screamed into the night, trying to make her voice work as she ran. 'Please. . . Stop shooting. . . You're shooting at a child. Please. . .'

She stared hopelessly above her at the dark tunnel of track. The moon was just starting to glimmer above the mountain ridge, casting an eerie shadow over the bush. Wacky hauled her forward, further and further, and then someone loomed ahead of them on the track, moving fast.

He didn't see them and Sally and Wacky were right in his path. The man hit Wacky in mid-gait, somersaulted forward, tried to twist as he fell and crumpled on to the ground with an oath of pain.

Sally took a step back. The man rolled over, swearing in agony, and his arm pointed straight up. Straight at Sally. The faint moonlight glinted on the blue metal of a gun.

A gun. . .

'I'm. . .I'm a doctor.'

Sally somehow managed to speak, but her voice was a croak. Her eyes were mesmerised by the gun. 'I'm here to find a lost child. Please. . .don't shoot. I can't hurt you.'

There was a long, long silence. Wacky stirred uneasily, Sally's hand still firm on his collar. The dog was clearly unsure of the situation. Was this man a threat? He tugged forward, anxious to be off again to his Lisa.

There was nothing Sally wanted more than to run, but she couldn't. Not while that thing pointed at her.

'Are you. . .? Are you hurt?' she whispered. 'Can I help you?'

'You shouldn't be here.' The man was still crumpled where he fell, his voice laced with pain. 'If you're here to interfere with the trees——'

'I'm not interested in the trees,' Sally interrupted him. 'There's a child here. I'm a local doctor. I just want to find her.'

'A child. . .'

'Lisa Maitland.' Somehow she had to take away this man's idea of Lisa and Sally as the enemy. 'She's ten years old and she's run away from home. I. . .I'm Sally Atchinson, a surgeon from Gundowring Hospital.'

'A surgeon. . .?'

'Yes.'

Silence. It went on and on, and the wicked little gun didn't move.

'You didn't hurt my brother, then?' he asked finally.

'Your brother?'

'My brother,' he repeated dully. 'The bloody protesters cost my brother his eyes with their damned nails. And they haven't been caught. Well, I'll make them sorry. . .'

'I think they're already sorry.' Sally took a deep breath. She fought for courage, trying desperately not to think of the dead Gary and the dreadfully hurt Melinda. Finally she took a step forward. 'I know that Dr Maitland—Lisa's father—was one of the doctors who fought to try and save your brother's sight. It's his little girl who's up here. Have you. . .? Have you hurt yourself badly?'

'My bloody ankle.' He cast her a final suspicious look, the gun still raised, but Sally was dropping to her knees, feeling his lower leg. 'Leave it alone. . .'

'It's broken,' Sally said gently. She could feel a compound fracture, sluggishly bleeding around the break. 'I'll have to help you back to the truck.'

'Like hell you will.' He raised his gun again. 'I should shoot you.'

'Maybe.' Sally closed her eyes, and when she opened them she'd found the courage she needed. 'But I didn't hurt your brother. It's true that I'm a doctor and it's true that there's a child lost up here. If you want to shoot me because of that then I guess you'd better get it over with quickly. Only, please. . .tell the police when they find you that the little girl they're looking for is still high on the mountain.'

Unless you shot her, she added silently to herself, her eyes not leaving his face.

'You're lying.'

'No.'

The silence stretched on and on. Wacky stood, whining impatiently beside Sally. Sally's spare hand still held his collar. He was her link to Lisa. If he went. . .

'The dog will take me to the little girl,' she said slowly. 'If. . . If you let me go.'

He closed his eyes, pain stretching across his face.

Sally grimaced. She couldn't leave him. The fracture had come through the skin.

'I've morphine in my bag—in the car,' she whispered. 'But. . . Will you hold the dog while I go? I don't think I can drag the dog back—away from where he wants to go.'

She was being a fool. To ask this man for help. . .

'If the dog disappears into the bush then I can't find the child,' she told him. 'But you need painkillers.'

He bit his lip, agony etched on his face. This could go either way.

'They'll know it was me who shot out the tyres. . .' he said slowly. 'If they find me.'

'I guess they will.' There was no point denying it.

'And they will find me—unless I make you take me away from here.'

Sally took a deep breath. 'I won't do that,' she said steadily. 'I have to find Lisa, but if you hold the dog then I'll get you morphine first. That way I can tell the police you did everything you could to help me. Or I'll walk away—and the only way you can stop me is a bullet in the back. And what sort of trouble will that land you in?'

'You'd never have the guts. . .'

'Please. . .' Sally whispered. 'I meant what I said. Please hold the dog.' She lifted the man's hand and twisted Wacky's collar under his fingers. 'Please. . .'

And she stood up, turned her back and walked away.

It was the longest few yards' walk of her life. The gun was still pointing at her. She could feel its aim, and the nerves were crawling up the small of her back.

Ten feet. Fifteen. . . And then the track twisted, the glimmer of moonlight faded behind the trees and Sally broke into a run.

And for the third time in her life she ran into Lloyd Neale.

This was no accident. It was intentional. He'd been

waiting in the gloom, his eyes accustomed to the dark
where Sally's eyes had changed focus with the brighter
moonlight. Now he knew exactly what he was doing
as he stepped out in front of her, catching her to him
and bringing her hand up to stifle her exclamation
as he did.

'Hush. . . Sally, it's me.'

Lloyd. . . Dear heaven, Lloyd. . .

His arms came around her and held her close, and
Sally's knees trembled and gave. She would have
fallen, but Lloyd was permitting no such thing.

'Dear love. . .' His lips were in her hair. 'My crazy
Sally. . . You crazy, crazy woman. . .'

'You decided to believe me. . .' She hardly knew
whether she whispered the words aloud. Lloyd must
have left at almost the same time as Sally. He must
have followed her. . . 'I thought you said I was silly. . .'
she whispered.

He had dragged her back, away from the track. Now
his hands held her close, trying to stop the tremors
sweeping through her body.

'Silly. . .' He shook his head. 'It's me who was silly,
my love, and I never knew how much. Where's Lisa?'

'I don't know. Lloyd, there were shots. . . She has
to be up on the ridge.'

'Then we go. I have a torch——'

'No!'

'Sally. . .'

'Lloyd, he has a compound fracture. I promised him
morphine.'

'And he threatened to shoot you. I've been listening.
I've nearly been going crazy with worry while I
listened. There's no choice now but to keep off the
track and go around him.'

'Wacky will bark when he hears us. He has
Wacky. . .' Sally cringed, her face falling on to Lloyd's
chest. 'Without Wacky we can't find Lisa.'

Lloyd was silent.

'You're not going back near him,' he finally muttered, but by his voice Sally knew he had already acknowledged that there was no choice.

'If I don't, then I don't get Wacky,' she whispered. 'If you go near him. . . Lloyd, he's so unstable. He could just go over the brink. I think. . .I think he trusts me.'

'We can wait. We can wait until Struan and the police arrive. I left a message that if Struan didn't find Lisa on the road then he should bring the police here.'

'And if the man's already shot Lisa. . . If she's bleeding somewhere up on the mountain. . . Lloyd, I have to get Wacky. And, unless you can think of a better way, the safest method is for me to give him morphine, wait until it takes effect, and then take Wacky quietly.'

'So you expect me to just stay here and wait while you face the gun again?' Lloyd grimaced. 'I can't do that.'

'No.' Sally didn't move her face from his chest. His arms holding her close were infinitely comforting. 'If you come back with me when I return with the morphine. . . If you slip through the bush at the side of the track when I get back to him, he'll think Wacky is barking because of my return. Then I could come on after the morphine takes effect and. . .and you'll be waiting.'

'If he doesn't shoot you. . .'

'He won't shoot me.' Her voice was much steadier than her heart, but there was no choice. She couldn't think of that hand. . .of that gun. . .

'You're the bravest——' Lloyd shook his head into the darkness. 'Sally. . .'

'Let's go.' Sally was already pulling away into the dark. 'Please, Lloyd, let's just go.'

They moved faster than Sally believed possible in the dark and with Lloyd's weak leg. It was Sally who

was slowest over the rough ground. Back at the cars—
Lloyd's now lined up next to Sally's—they grabbed
Sally's bag and ran back the way they had come, their
hands linked in the dark. When the track curved round
to where the injured man lay, Lloyd pulled Sally off
the track and roughly kissed her.

'Know that I love you,' he growled. 'Know that I've
been a damned fool. . .'

'Hush.' She laid a finger on his lips, took her courage
in both hands and left him in the dark.

As she had expected, Wacky greeted her with
exuberance, barking fiercely, and if the dog was looking to the side of the track, to where Lloyd was feeling
his way carefully through the undergrowth, the man
was too intent on the pain in his leg to notice. He
was still holding Wacky for all he was worth. Sally
administered morphine and, by the light of the torch
from her bag, checked the leg more thoroughly. The
bleeding had slowed and there was nothing else she
could do until she had the man back into Casualty.

The gun was no longer in sight. Sally moved to the
man's head, released Wacky's collar from his fingers
and took the logger's hand in hers.

'The pain will ease soon. Morphine works fast.
And. . .thank you for holding Wacky,' she told him
gently. She wouldn't let herself think that this man
might have shot Lisa. She would only think that he'd
held the dog—that he'd tried to help.

That he *hadn't* shot Lisa. . .

'I wouldn't hurt the kid. . .' It was as if the man
had read her thoughts. He flinched as he stirred on
the hard ground. 'Don't sweat on the kid. I saw someone and I fired over her head. She screamed and. . .
Well, I decided whoever it was I'd scared enough. Hell,
I didn't want a repeat of what happened last time.'

'Last time?'

'Those two young fools in the car. I caught them

putting more nails into the trees—more! When they'd already done so much damage! Logging was my brother's livelihood and they cost him his sight. I was just trying to scare them. And that's all. . . That's all I was trying to do this time——' His voice broke and Sally tightened her grip on his hand.

'Don't worry,' she said. 'Help will be here soon. And maybe, if you're honest, things will start looking a bit better.'

'I'll have to go to court.'

'Yes. But you didn't mean to hurt the kids, and you've helped me.'

He clutched her hand tighter, and Sally mentally counted the moments until the morphine took effect. She could feel the second it did by the slackening of tension in his hand.

'I have to go,' she whispered. She released the remaining grip on her hand.

'To find the kid?'

'To find Lisa.'

'Yeah. . .' His voice was drifting. 'You do that. . . And, Doc. . .?'

'Yes?'

He fumbled underneath him and the gun was in his hand again, this time being pointed at her handle-first.

'You take this. In case. . . In case you meet any bloody muggers on the mountain.'

'I'll do that.'

The relief Sally felt was almost overwhelming. Now Struan and the police, hurrying up the track to search for them, would come upon an injured man without a weapon. Sally hadn't allowed herself to think of the consequences of leaving him with a gun, but now. . .

Now she took Wacky's collar more firmly in her hand and straightened.

'I'll see you soon,' she promised. She stood for a brief moment, looking down at this man who'd caused

such tragedy, and then she turned and walked the way
Lloyd had already gone.

As soon as she rounded the next bend in the track
she lifted the gun and tossed it into the bush at the
side of the road. She didn't have a clue how to unload
it, and if she stumbled and the thing went off. . .

Then she broke into a run.

Twenty yards further on Lloyd was waiting. They
didn't speak, just linked hands and kept running,
Wacky towing them through the dark.

And three hundred yards later they found Lisa. Or,
at least, they found where Lisa had been.

Wacky hauled them up to the edge of the ridge and
then stood, staring anxiously over the edge into the
darkness.

'Lisa?' Lloyd called, and then his voice faded as he
realised what lay ahead.

Sally stopped dead behind Wacky, one hand in
Wacky's collar and the other in Lloyd's grasp. Their
hands were linked but each of the three—man, woman
and dog—seemed alone with a nightmare. A cliff-edge
and silence.

Wacky whimpered.

'Dear God. . .' It was Sally's fearful whisper. She
thought back to that scream.

Lloyd cupped his hands around his mouth and yelled
once again. There was no need to be quiet now. Even
if the injured logger could hear, there was nothing he
could do.

Nothing.

Wacky stirred uneasily and whimpered again.

'Lisa. . .' Sally was standing with horror filling her
heart. How steep was the drop? She couldn't see.
There was nothing. . .

'L-Lloyd. . .'

The word was hardly a whisper coming up out of
the darkness. It was a creeping, fearful breath, and it

came from right under where they stood.

'Lisa!' Lloyd was lying full-length on his stomach, his torch pointing over the ridge. 'Lisa, sweetheart, are you OK? Where the hell are you?'

'I'm down here.' Still the fearful, breathless whisper. 'I don't know. . . I'm on a little ledge. I don't know where the edge is. I can't see and I'm scared. . .'

'I'm coming down, Lisa. Hold on.'

Like Lloyd, Sally had dropped to lie full-length on the ground. Now she swivelled in horror to Lloyd. 'Lloyd. . . You can't. . .'

'Can't go down? What are you suggesting, Sally? That we leave her there?'

'No.' Sally's torch was picking up the steep slope between the top of the ridge and where Lisa lay. Their lightly powered torches could just make out a still, pale shape, twenty feet down. The drop wasn't quite vertical but it was as near straight down as made no difference. A few footholds in the crumbling earth, maybe. . . .

'If she moves. . .' Lloyd was pushing his torch into the waist of his trousers. 'We can't leave her there, Sally. It could be half an hour or more before help comes. And if she falls. . . If she falls while I stay here and do nothing. . .'

'But I'll go.' Sally caught at his hands. 'Lloyd, you can't. . . Your leg. . .'

'My leg is fine. You told me so yourself.'

'I said it could be better.' Sally was crying with fright. 'I didn't say it was normal.'

'You said. . .' Lloyd put his hands on her shoulders. They were kneeling at the edge of the cliff, the moonlight shining on their faces. 'You said I was afraid of dragons. Well, I'm damned if I'll let the woman I love face dragons on my behalf. And Lisa. . . Well, Lisa's one special dragon.'

'I'll tell her you said that.' Sally gave a shaken laugh

and touched his face with her finger. 'Oh, Lloyd. . .
Oh, Lloyd, be careful.'

'I'll be careful,' he promised. He kissed her swiftly
on the lips. 'All of a sudden, I've got a heap to be
careful for. If you forgive me. . . If you forgive me
for ever doubting you, then. . .'

CHAPTER TWELVE

SOMEHOW, he made it. Days later, when Sally and Lloyd came up to look in daylight, to retrieve a remembered gun and to inspect the climb Lloyd had managed to perform, Sally could only shudder. Somehow, though, he had managed to get down the twenty feet to where Lisa lay. Sally had heard his grunt of satisfaction and then quiet voices from below. Finally. . .

'Sally?'

'Y-yes. . .' She had been staring over the drop, her torch shining pathetically into the darkness in an attempt to give Lloyd more light.

'She's OK, Sally. She's a bit bruised and a lot frightened, but she's OK.'

Sally closed her eyes. She pulled back from the ledge, placed her arms around Wacky's neck and held on as if her life depended on it.

'Sally. . . Are you there?'

'Y-yes.'

'I'm not going to move until help arrives,' Lloyd called. 'The ledge is about twelve inches wide, and as far as I can see the drop beneath us is frightening. We stay where we are until Struan and the police arrive.'

'I. . .I'll go and guide them here.'

'You stay where you are.' It was an urgent command. 'They'll see the cars and figure out where we are. You're not to risk going down that track again. If one of the logger's mates arrives. . . You stay where you are.'

'Yes, Lloyd. . .'

So, nearly an hour later, when it seemed half the

population of Gundowring arrived, headed by a frantic Struan and with people armed with ropes and lanterns, and State Emergency Service volunteers trained in mountain rescue, and goodness knows what else besides, Sally was still perched where she was, pointing helplessly down.

Even then it took fifteen minutes to bring Lisa and Lloyd to the top of the ridge. Lisa came first, harnessed to the front of an SES volunteer. She was gathered into her father's arms and held close, but Sally hardly saw. Her eyes were on the ledge, waiting for her Lloyd.

And then he came, harnessed safely, but manoeuvring the tenuous footholds by himself. Willing arms lifted him over the edge and rid him of his harness. Voices were congratulating him, but Lloyd had eyes only for Sally.

Only for his Sally.

Somehow she was in his arms. Sally didn't remember moving, or Lloyd coming to her, but she was being held tighter than she had ever been held in her life and the men and lanterns and smiles and laughter faded to nothing. There was only each other.

No marriage vows could have cemented them to each other more firmly than that moment.

With this love, I thee wed. . .

Afterwards, when the commonplace had finally intruded on their union, when the police had taken their statements, when the ambulancemen had taken the injured logger back to the hospital and when Struan had thanked and congratulated and finally teased the pair of them, and then had taken his daughter home to bed, Sally and Lloyd sat on under the huge gum-trees—Lisa's trees—gazing out over the moonlit hills to the distant sea.

Above their heads the warm wind rustled in the mighty gums. A link to the past. A link to the future. . .

'She was right to try and save them,' Sally said softly, a tinge of sadness rushing in at the thought of their splendour being taken.

'I tell you what,' Lloyd said softly, 'I have this terrific little retirement fund saved up. I believe you've been a little scathing about my retirement plans in the past, Dr Atchinson. How about I use some of my money to have the timber on the mountain ridge preserved?'

'Could you?' Sally turned within the circle of his arms and looked wonderingly into his dark eyes.

'I've always thought that, in order to retire, a man should have a place to retire to.' Lloyd kissed her lightly on the lips. 'This seems a great place for retirement.' He kissed her again, this time more deeply. And then again. . .'Only. . . Only a man has to have someone to retire with,' he said at last. 'Would you retire here with me, my Sally? My dearest love?'

'Wh-when?' Sally's voice trembled, but she wasn't cold. She had never felt warmer in her life. 'When were you thinking of retiring?'

He smiled, and pulled her down to lie full-length on the underblanket of soft, scented gum-leaves. Above their heads the stars twinkled through the canopy of branches, and from somewhere in the distance a night-bird called. It ought to be a nightingale, Sally thought hazily. What a pity we don't have them in Australia.

'If we're going to retire, my Sally——' Lloyd smiled again as he took her in his arms and held her close '—how about now? How about right now?'

It sounded just fine to Sally.

Christmas Journeys

4 new short romances all wrapped up in 1 sparkling volume.

Join four delightful couples as they journey home for the festive season—and discover the true meaning of Christmas...that love is the best gift of all!

A Man To Live For - Emma Richmond

Yule Tide - Catherine George

Mistletoe Kisses - Lynsey Stevens

Christmas Charade - Kay Gregory

Available: November 1995 **Price: £4.99**

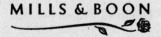

MILLS & BOON

MILLS & BOON

CHRISTMAS CRACKERS

**A cracker of a gift pack full of
Mills & Boon goodies. You'll find...**

Passion—in *A Savage Betrayal* by Lynne Graham
A beautiful baby—in *A Baby for Christmas* by Anne McAllister
A Yuletide wedding—in *Yuletide Bride* by Mary Lyons
A Christmas reunion—in *Christmas Angel* by Shannon Waverly

Special Christmas price of 4 books
for £5.99 (usual price £7.96)

Published: November 1995

*Available from WH Smith, John Menzies, Volume One, Forbuoys, Martins,
Tesco, Asda, Safeway and other paperback stockists.*

 **WIN**

A years supply of Mills & Boon Romances — absolutely free!

Would you like to win a years supply of heartwarming and passionate romances? Well, you can and they're FREE! All you have to do is complete the wordsearch puzzle below and send it to us by 30th April 1996. The first 5 correct entries picked after that date will win a years supply of Mills & Boon Romance novels (six books every month – worth over £100). What could be easier?

STOCKHOLM	PARIS	HELSINKI	ANKARA
REYKJAVIK	LONDON	ROME	AMSTERDAM
COPENHAGEN	PRAGUE	VIENNA	OSLO
MADRID	ATHENS	LIMA	

N	O	L	S	O	P	A	R	I	S
E	Q	U	V	A	F	R	O	K	T
G	C	L	I	M	A	A	M	N	O
A	T	H	E	N	S	K	E	I	C
H	L	O	N	D	O	N	H	S	K
N	S	H	N	R	I	A	O	L	H
E	D	M	A	D	R	I	D	E	O
P	R	A	G	U	E	U	Y	H	L
O	A	M	S	T	E	R	D	A	M
C	R	E	Y	K	J	A	V	I	K

Please turn over for details on how to enter ➡

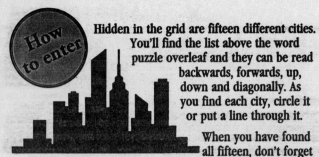

How to enter

Hidden in the grid are fifteen different cities. You'll find the list above the word puzzle overleaf and they can be read backwards, forwards, up, down and diagonally. As you find each city, circle it or put a line through it.

When you have found all fifteen, don't forget to fill in your name and address in the space provided below and pop this page in an envelope (you don't need a stamp) and post it today. Hurry — competition ends 30th April 1996.

Mills & Boon Capital Wordsearch
FREEPOST
Croydon
Surrey
CR9 3WZ

Are you a Reader Service Subscriber?   Yes ❑   No ❑

Ms/Mrs/Miss/Mr _____

Address _____

_____

—————————— Postcode ——————————

One application per household.

You may be mailed with other offers from other reputable companies as a result of this application. If you would prefer not to receive such offers, please tick box. ❑   COMP495
                                                                        D